IT GETS BETTER

The story of a troubled family

Yasir Mazhar

2

IT GETS BETTER

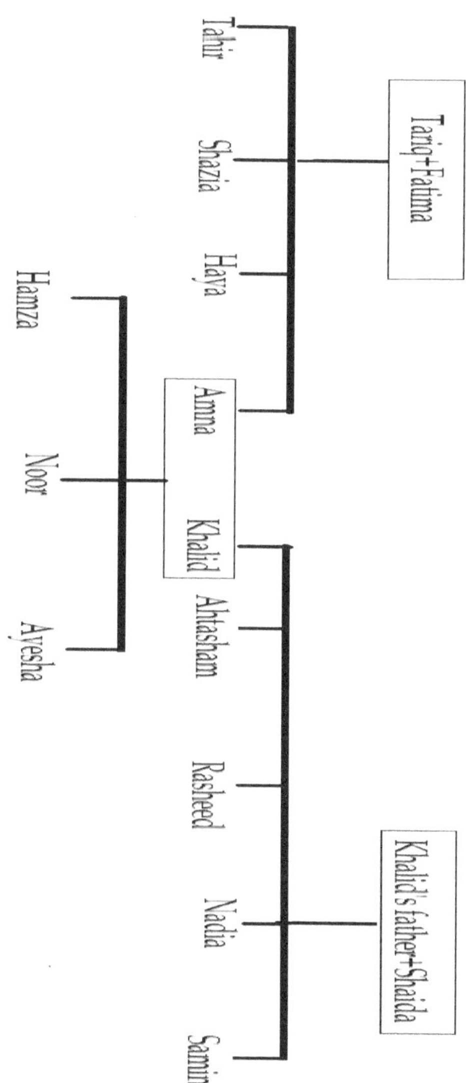

PROLOGUE

"But I can't!" said Tariq. "But I love you Tariq! I love you; I have loved you all my life! You can't do this to me. What is it that she has and I don't? I can change myself; I will do whatever you'll say Tariq, just make me yours. That is all I want" cried Shaida. Tariq said, "I know you love me and I respect that but I love Fatima and she loves me; we both are in love and I am loyal towards her. We are going to get married in a few days; you need to stop this!" "Just tell her you don't want to marry her and then we can get married!" Shaida yelled. Tariq forbid her from saying another word as he walked out of the room.

Shaida loved Tariq since she had heard the word 'love'. She always knew she was his; she claimed him as the king of her heart. She had never thought that this was going to happen. Fatima was Shaida's childhood friend and Shaida felt like Fatima stabbed her in her back while shaking her hand by falling in love with

Tariq. Fatima did not have any choice; no one can control who they love and who they don't

but Shaida could not understand that. She decided that if she could not get Tariq than neither will Fatima. She watched the love of her life get married with her childhood friend. It was devastating for her, she was not going to let go of this. She had to take revenge on Fatima for doing this. Years passed. Shaida got married and moved to another city. She had some children; three boys and two girls. She had still not forgotten what she had to do to Fatima. She had a plan. She traveled to Tariq's house to 'meet' the couple. To her surprise, Tariq had had four children; a son and three daughters. They all were very young, some of them did not even know how to properly talk or walk. They were really cute.

Shaida knew what she had to do. She decided she was going to poison her own childhood friend who now had to take care of all her little angels but Shaida did not care about that. All that she wanted was revenge. She had to think of something that would not get her in trouble. She knew what to do. She had heard the story of a family that died after accidentally drinking milk which had been boiled with a dead garden lizard inside of it and no one knew why they had died until their autopsy was done. She knew Tariq was not rich enough to afford an autopsy and also he could not bear his wife being cut apart to see why she died. It was a brilliant idea. Shaida was neither grossed out by lizards nor scared of them. She went outside and caught herself a lizard in a plastic bag after a long time of searching for it. She killed it by hitting it against the counter while it was still in the plastic bag. She also kept a close eye if anyone was watching her. She then put the whole dead bleeding lizard in the boiling pot of milk. After awhile, she poured some milk into a cup and served it to Fatima. She poisoned her own childhood friend; the friend that played with her as a child, the friend that supported her, the friend that motivated her to succeed as a child, the friend who could never have wanted any harm to come to Shaida, she poisoned her childhood friend. Fatima died, leaving all her little children under the protection of her love, Tariq. Shaida had succeeded in her mission but she still wanted more from Tariq. She planed something that was sure to be the end of Tariq. Tariq was the single father of four children; Tahir, Shazia, Haya and Amna whereas Shaida had a total of five children; Rasheed, Khalid, Ahtasham, Samina and Nadia.

CHAPTER ONE

At the peak of this little argument, Amna told everyone hesitantly that she did not want to marry the man her father had selected for her. She was not completely certain but she had a feeling that he was not right for her. She told this to her family and her father said, "He is a good rich man, he has his own car and a white collar job, what else do you want!" "I do not want to hear anything else from you" her elder brother ordered. "If you are doing this because you are dating someone else, I am going to murder you and him! So it is best that you marry this man" her brother said angrily as he thought that Amna was not marrying this man just because she was dating someone else but something that he did not notice was that she was too young to do so and also a little to innocent as well. "Stop it now! I know Amna is a good girl, she knows that girls of our family don't do things like this, I know that she is going to understand that we only want her best" said her father nicely as he stopped his son.

Amna had two sisters and a brother. Her eldest sister Shazia was quite selfish, bold whereas her younger sister, Haya, was really clumsy as a child as well as a married adult. Their brother, Tahir, was strict but caring and loving in his own unique way. Amna, alongside her siblings, was raised by her father only. The father loved his daughters a lot more than he loved his son. He treated all three of them in the best way he could. They all had a strong bond of affection between them. Her mother passed away when they all were all under ten years of age. This left the father alone who loved his wife deeply. He tried to play the role of their mother as well as their father and valued them the most but still could not fill the blank space in their children's hearts; the blank space that is supposed to be filled by a mother's pure affection, care and unconditional love.

They lived in a small, undeveloped and not so populated town. The father owned a small house with only three rooms and a small but clean kitchen and a small washroom. The small, old shed like house was located in a narrow street near by the local market. The house was almost half a century old and needed a lot of renovations but due to the less pay of the father, it was almost impossible for him to make any betterment in the house. From leaking taps and broken windows to a leaking roof and broken, hanging doors, everything needed fixing but alas, the father's pay did not allow that. This was a family where children had to wait for days to get their school fee from their father which was a very small amount; but still it was quite a lot for them.

The children made sure that the hard earned money went to the right cause and so they studied as hard as they could. This hard work and their intelligence were the reasons for their peak performance at school.

Amna was great at everything; cooking, dressing, art every single thing a sixteen year old girl can learn and much more. She grew up ahead of time, time taught her to be much more of an adult than a girl her age could possibly be. She was humorous and so full of life. She was always the most helpful and supportive to be around out of all her siblings. Everyone loved her because of her amiable, solicitous, obliging and forbearing personality. She was a rose bud, full of wishes to completely bloom but she did not know what was decided for her in the future by her fate.

She was around sixteen and was going through high school. She would wake up in the morning before anyone did just to prepare breakfast for herself and everyone else in the house. It was Shazia's duty to prepare breakfast for everyone but Shazia would take an unfair advantage of Amna's helpful and obedient nature and always order her to do all the things she had to do. Another casual morning, she woke up and as per usual, prepared breakfast for everyone and then started getting ready for school. When it was time for Fajar, (a way of worshipping that Muslims around the world practice) she woke everyone up and told them that breakfast was ready. Her father woke up, washed his face and kissed her on her forehead and wished for the best of her future. She woke up her sisters and brother as well.

After offering the Fajar prayer, they all sat down to eat breakfast. The time passed well as they finished eating their breakfast whilst their father delivered a small moral lecture. The siblings got up and said their goodbyes as they left for school. Their father kissed each of his children on their forehead as they left the house. The father then, geared up to go to work; his job was to lift and carry the heavy sacs of raw material around where needed at a factory. He would sometimes do some other tasks as well to earn some extra cash. It was a laborious job but he was determined to educate his children so they did not have to suffer like he was. He used to come back home at almost seven in the evening but sometimes he would arrive home by eight or nine at night.

The children's day went fine at school and now it was time to leave. They left the school and came home. The other siblings went to their same room while Amna went to the kitchen. When she passed in front of her father's room, she saw his work cloths hanging inside on the wall. She thought it was weird that he had come home so early. She peeked inside his room to see if he was there but to her surprise, he was not. She heard some people, alongside her father, talking from the living room. She thought she should prepare tea for her father and every one with him in that room. Judging by the amount of different voices she heard, she assumed that there were almost three people in the room including her father. She prepared tea for them and took it to them. There were two young men, one bearded and the other having a small mustache. Both of them were dressed well in neat suits. She served the tea and left the room to go get some rest in her room (which she shared with all her three siblings). She saw that Haya and Shazia were resting on the small bed so she decided to nap on the carpet.

When she got up, she went to her father and asked him about those people because she saw them for the first time. Amna knew all her father's friends very well and they were not one of them. Her father told her that they came here to ask for your hand in marriage. She blushed as she looked down and smiled lightly. She asked her father hesitantly in a low voice, "My hand?" and then ran out of the room laughing lightly like a rose she was.

The next day, those people visited again. This time, the person for whom they had asked Amna's hand for was also with them. She prepared the best tea she could for them (when a person asks for a girl's hand in marriage in Pakistan and some other countries, it is a usual custom for the girl to serve them tea) and served it to them. She assumed that the third new person with them was her supposed husband to be. Anyway, when they were gone, she confirmed it from her father and realized that she was absolutely right. Her father further told her that it was final that they were going to get married soon. He was a rich, well respected man. He asked her if she did not have any problem with it and as expected; Amna said she was indeed happy. Her father told her that she was going to meet her future husband in just a few days. That night, the sisters sat together and talked about how Amna felt all night long and all Amna did was smile or blush.

A few days passed and finely, Amna's husband to be came to see her. They sat face to face for the very first time. After talking for a while, Amna realized that something was off. She asked him about his age and he told her that he was around twenty two. She told him that he looked older that he said he was. He told him that he already knew what her name was and his name was Khalid.

Anyway, they left after fixing the date for their marriage. Amna asked her father about the age of Khalid because she just knew he was not as young as he said to be. Her father told her that he was around thirty. This surprised Amna who was told that Khalid was twenty two.

She told her father about all what she thought and her father just ignored it all by saying," oh he must be joking". Tahir said," And what if he is a little older to you, he is rich, he is respected by everyone in the society, has his own house and a car. I don't think you should have any problem with marrying him." Amna agreed with a heavy heart. She just did not have the courage to take a stand and tell everyone that she did not want to marry him for several reasons other than the fact that she was only sixteen and he was around thirty. She tried to convince her father and brother but her brother either strictly forbid her from further arguing on the topic or her father would nicely sit her down and convince her that Khalid was the man of her dreams. Maybe nobody understood that they were going to make the decision on which Amna's future and rest of the life depended on.

Amna further got to know that Khalid lived in another city so if she was going to marry her, she had to agree on not seeing her beloved family not very often or possibly ever again. The biggest mistake Amna's father made was not actually going to Khalid's house and seeing his house for himself. He did not do so because he knew Khalid's eldest brother Rasheed pretty well (the same brother who came to Amna's house and asked for her hand in marriage for his younger brother and said that they were wealthy people) and he trusted him for what he said. He also was not able to do so because of his financial states.

Khalid had four siblings; two sisters and two brothers. Both his sisters, Shabana and Nadia were younger to him. However Nadia was the youngest among them all. His two brothers were Rashid and Ahtasham. Ahtasham was younger to Khalid and was the same age as Nadia. Rasheed was the eldest among them all. Khalid's siblings did not love Khalid as siblings are supposed to. Nadia and Ahtasham however loved him dearly but did not get the same love back from him. Khalid was the only one who earned for the family. Rasheed had married the love of his life against his mother's will but that did not bother him. Nadia and Ahtasham were both studying and almost the same age as Amna. Khalid had to go to another city to earn on a weekly basis. Khalid seemed like a very nice person and even promised that he would not restrict her from getting education after their marriage. Amna was now satisfied and knew that she was going to marry the man of her dreams. He was nice, rich and caring. For once she did not care if she was too young to get married to a thirty year old man.

All her concerns were alleviated when Khalid told her father that he would allow Amna to visit her family once every month. It was time to start shopping for the wedding. Amna was beyond delighted. According to a custom, the bride to be can either chose between shopping with her husband to be or her sisters. Amna thought that it would be great to spend some quality time with her sisters before she got married and moved to another city. The bride's family has to prepare a set of cloths, jewelry and makeup items and even furniture to send with the bride to her new home. It was a difficult decision to move away from her family to another city but she just knew it was worth it. Khalid told her that he was going to shop for his wedding dress by himself in his home city. Amna thought it was fine since she also chose to shop with her family. Despite Amna's father's less pay, he still allowed his daughters to the dresses of their choice without caring about the price but Amna still cared a lot for her father and knew it won't be easy for him to get some extra cash so she bought everything in a low price rang. Her dresses did not have to be expensive to look gorgeous; she looked absolutely stunning wearing the low cost dresses. Her sense of dressing was highly commendable so it was no wonder that she had picked out the gems as her dresses. The furniture was going to be bought by her brother, Tahir. He did a great job as well in picking out the furniture for her sister. This set of clothing, furniture and makeup items are usually referred to as "Jahez". Jahez is a symbol of love and affection the bride's family. It is also to symbolize the wealth of the bride's family so it was no wonder that Amna's family did their best to choose the items for Amna's Jahez. The dresses for her engagement and wedding were also carefully chosen by Amna and her sisters. Amna's eldest sister Shazia was a rebel and did what satisfied her and did not care about anyone else. Amna was complete opposite of that. Shazia had married the man she loved dearly. Her father had not allowed

Shazia to marry him but his sayings did not change her decision. Shazia had to go back to her home after a day or two so mostly the shopping had to be done by Amna and her younger sister, Haya. Amna was going to get married in a few weeks so the family decided to send as much time as they could with her. Shabana came to stay with her family for a week before her sister, Amna got married. It was just like when the sisters were young, sleeping in the same room and talking the night away. All this bliss and renewed past memories gave them joy but also made their hearts heavy by the thought that this was not going to happen rarely in the future after Amna moves to another city.

CHAPTER TWO

It was time. Amna was going to get married to the man of her dreams. Amna was supremely joyous on this day. This was the day that Amna and her family had to go to Khalid's home city to attend the wedding. Khalid had booked an extravagant wedding hall for their wedding. This added to Amna's joy and delight even more and beyond thought. Despite their enchantment about Amna's wedding, her family was still blue because of the thought that they had to let go of their beloved angel. They had to get ready for the occasion earlier because they had to reach there earlier than anyone else. Amna did not get her makeup done neither did she wear her bridal cloths because she was going to do all that when she would reach the Wedding hall. They started their journey in the train and got there in almost an hour. Her family went directly to the wedding hall while Amna went to the beauty parlor to get her makeup done.

Her family gasped to see the baronial splendor of the wedding hall that Khalid had booked for the wedding. Her father was satisfied to know that he was marrying his daughter in the right people. They had just entered the hall when they say Khalid's family dressed in beautiful expensive dresses standing near the main stage. They start to come towards Amna's family who were dressed in average dresses, to greet them.

Haya went to talk to Ahtasham and Nadia because they were the only ones that were anywhere near her age. Haya was still younger to Nadia and Ahtasham so their mentality was not the same but similar. After talking to them for a while, Haya became good friends with both of the siblings because of their amiable personalities and welcoming natures and then for the rest of the time Haya stayed with them both other than the times she was with her sister, the bride.

Shazia went to talk to someone her age which turned out to be Shabana. Shabana looked at Shazia, rolled her eyes and looked away, ignoring Shazia completely. Shazia was herself confident, independent and bold so when Shabana showed her some bad attitude, it did not take time for Shazia to get mad but before she said something, she kept it in mind that it was her younger sister's wedding. But even that thought did not keep her from taunting Shabana sarcastically after a while or two. Shabana did not hold back either from taunting Shazia. Smiling and taunting, it was like giving each other the most luscious poison that would slowly burn them from the inside. It did not take much time until they both went their own different ways.

Tahir went to hang out with Rasheed. Rasheed was a proud narcissist and thought of every one other than him as an inferior being, even his siblings. Tahir started the conversation by talking about where exactly was Khalid's house. Rasheed replied," Oh it's near the market in a great and beautiful location. It's really peaceful and safe where the house is. It definitely stands out from the rest of the houses. I am sure that Amna would love her new home. By the way, what have you included in the Jahez?" Tahir told him a long list of items that he had included in the Jahez. They continued their conversation talking about the furniture in the Jahez and some other things.

Amna's father and Khalid's father were sitting together and as every parent does, were bragging about their children. Khalid's mother told him that Khalid had his own business and was living a successful life. She told Amna's father that his income was around fifty thousand rupees (almost five hundred dollars). Amna's father was satisfied and tranquil that he was on the right path. He told Khalid's mother that Amna was the most helpful, obedient and religious one out of all his four children. He confirmed Khalid's age from his mother and he got to know that his exact age was thirty six years. For a moment he thought that it was wrong to marry his little sixteen year old girl to a mature thirty six year old man but then again forgot about it when Khalid's mother told him about all the qualities Khalid had.

Finely the time came the Beautiful bride and the handsome bridegroom walked in the door forming the most absolutely stunning couple. Everyone stood up and clapped as the couple walked in and approached the stage. Tears rolled down both Amna's and her family members' eyes when they saw each other. Amna lightly smiled as Khalid held her hand helped her get up on the stage. She sat down on the love seat with her future husband like a princess. They both turned their faces towards the people and smiled. Khalid pulled out a ring case and looked at Amna with affection as he smiled. He opened the case and put Amna's ring finger through the ring. Everyone in the Wedding hall started clapping as Amna shed a tear of joy and her family members joined her. She called her father up on the stage quietly and hugged him as tight as she could as she finely let it all out and cried as much as she wanted without caring for her makeup. Her father consoled her as he quietly he a tear himself as well.

Amna's family was gloomy because they knew that she was going away and they were only going to be able to see her once a month. Though she was getting married to the man of her dreams, it was still a difficult decision to make to leave her family and move to another city: especially at this young of an age. But she thought it was all worth it. Amna called all her family members on the sage one by one and hugged each one of them out of her intimacy for her family.

The meal commenced and everyone's mouth watered to see the wide range of moreish dishes from all around the world served in front of them. It was confirmed, Khalid's family was wealthy but that was not the only thing that mattered. The thing that mattered was how much Khalid and his family loved Amna. They were desperately waiting for Amna to become a part of their family. The meal was served in the form of a buffet so everyone had to get up from their seats and get their food but it was worth it.

The waiters got some part of every dish in a separate plate and took it to the bride and bridegroom. Amna had never seen such food, being a girl belonging to a poor family; she had never tasted international foods. For awhile, Amna hesitated to taste any of the food that was in front of her. She looked over to Khalid who was enjoying his meal in the best way possible so she thought it would help to ask him about which food tastes better than the rest. She slowly turned to Khalid and said, "Um, could you please tell me which food out of these tastes best? I have never had anything thing like these my whole life. It would also be very kind of you if you tell me about the names of these since you know about these dishes from the time you were born. I would love to learn about these dishes." Khalid chuckled as he thought for a while of what to answer to Amna's question before saying," Well, uh…, this one is from Italy" as he pointed towards a bowl of hot tomato soup. He clearly did not know what those dishes were or where they were from but he continued to tell her about all the knowledge he had about those dishes. The one correct thing he did tell Amna was what tasted good and what did not; anyone could do that just by tasting the food.

Amna started to eat some of the food gradually keeping in mind that she was wearing makeup. Because of the fact that she was wearing makeup for the very first time, she was very careful not to smudge any of it and so she had a hard time eating anything and definitely took a long time to finish it too. She was not even done with eating half of her food when Khalid was done eating all of his food. He looked over at Amna's plate and said," Hey can I have some of your food?" Amna being a generous and kind young lady had no problem with sharing her food with her new husband. Khalid told Amna that he was just really hungry because he had not eaten much in the past days due to burden of office work. Amna told him that it was completely fine and she had no problem sharing her food with him, she even said that he could take more if he had wanted. She said this and the next thing she knew was that Khalid had taken some more food off her plate and eaten it. This did not bother Amna at all; in fact, she thought that it was amazing that she was now married to such an industrious man. Just the thought that she was now married made her beyond enchanted but the thought that she was going to be away from her family for a long time made her highly forlorn.

According to a custom in Pakistan, the quests at a wedding either give the newlywed couple a gift usually a home appliance or give them money so the couple can set up their new home. One by one, the guests came up on stage and kept either an envelope on the table in front of the couple or told them what they bought for them. Most of the people gave them money because it is a wide concept that it is better to give someone money instead of a gift so that they could buy whatever they need with that money. It also seems logical to give someone money instead of gifting them something they might not have required. Everyone gave them envelopes having money in them but it was quite difficult for anyone to see how much money the envelopes contained but Amna was neither concerned about how much money they got because she was not someone who was hungry for money; all she wanted in life was love and affection.

Amna was sitting head down, smiling with Khalid. Songs played in the background as the lights in the hall shifted color. People asked the camera man to click their photos with the bride and the bridegroom. Because Amna had cried earlier, her makeup was not of the best kind but it was not too off either. Most of the guests were the people who were either the relatives of Khalid or his friends. The only people from Amna's side were her sisters, her brother and her father and a few of her friends.

According to another custom, the sisters and the friends of the bride hide one of the shoes of the bridegroom and trade it for money. Their goal is to ask for a price as high as possible for a single shoe. It is meant to be a fun custom that helps in bonding. Amna's sisters took one of Khalid's shoes when he went to offer his prayer in a room inside the marriage hall. They then hid the single shoe under one of the tables. The goal of the bridegroom's friends is to lower the asked price of the shoe otherwise find it themselves. Most of the times they prefer to lower the price instead of looking for the shoe themselves. Khalid walked out of the room and instantly realized that Amna's sisters or her friends had hidden his shoe. He smiled and walked to the stage bare footed. He sat down and politely asked Amna's sisters," How much would I have to pay to get my shoe back?" Amna's sisters and her friends decided the price among them and told him that it would be twenty thousand rupees for his shoe. As the custom would have gone, Khalid's friends tried to convince Amna's sisters and her friends to lower the price and they succeeded to some extent. The price that was fixed was thirteen thousand rupees for the shoe. Khalid pulled out bills of thousands out of his pocket, counted and gave Amna's friends and her sisters thirteen thousand rupees. He then joked about it saying," Look Amna, it has not even been a day since I have married you and I already have lost thirteen thousand rupees." Everyone laughed as Amna's sisters, friends and Khalid's friends moved down from the stage.

The wedding continued and Amna started enjoying it until, it was finely time for her family to leave. All the customs had been done and now it was time to end the day. Amna looked at her father for the last time as tears rolled down her face. Haya got emotional and started crying uncontrollably. Shazia controlled her emotions but still her eyes filled with tears. Her father sniveled as he wiped away his tears and walked towards his daughter and said," This is going to be your new home Amna. Show them all what I taught you. I won't be along your side from now on to tell you what is wrong and what is right; it's up to you to make all your decisions from now own. I just know you would never do anything that would disappoint me. It might be a little difficult for you to fit in because of our difference in financial states but I have seen how much Khalid and his family love you. I pray for your eternal joy, Amen." Haya ran toward Amna and hugged her as tight as she could. It was like she was never going to let go of her sister. Shazia gracefully walked to Amna looked her in her eyes and stated crying as she hugged he beloved sister. Tahir, even, being a masculine person, could not help himself from shedding a tear to see his sister for possibly the last time. Amna was crying like a little child, sobbing, it was like she was going to faint. She sat her family down in a cab and said her final good bye as the cab driver drove away. She wiped away her tears wiping most of her makeup along with them. Khalid hugged her and told her that she was going to be touch with her family very often. Amna was happy to have married such a gentle man. They both smiled at each other as Khalid once again hugged her.

Khalid's mother came along with the rest of his family and told him that it was time to go. Nadia and Ahtasham were Amna's age fellows and so they kept on talking to Amna all the way home. Amna thought of Shabana, Khalid's sister who was elder to Nadia but younger to him, as a reserve introvert because Shabana barely talked to Amna on the way but Amna tried not to set up a wrong conception about anyone and so she thought that Shabana was not talking much because she was tired and maybe that's how she was. Anyway Ahtasham and Nadia were so excited that they did not let Amna notice anything else other than what they said.

CHAPTER THREE

The ride took almost half an hour to end. The two cars in which sat Amna, Khalid and his family stopped on a wide road. It was about eight o' clock and there was quiet some amount of people and cars moving on the road. The street lights were switched on. They got off the cars and Amna asked," Why have we stopped here?" Khalid replied," Uh, well you'll see." He paid the driver as the drivers drove away. She again asked him," I thought those were your cars?" He did not reply so Amna waited patiently. She was confused at this moment. She was dressed in a bridal gown and standing in the middle of a busy road. It was really weird for Amna so she asked," Is your house in this area? If yes then why are we not going to your house yet, I feel awkward." Khalid's mother said ,"Have patience young lady! We are going there in just a moment, you can see for yourself where the house is then." Amna was shocked to hear her mother-in-law speak in this manner to her. She again assumed that it must be because they all were really tired so she decided not to ask more questions. Khalid told her that his house was nearby so they had to walk to it. Amna had no problem with this but the only problem was that she was wearing a bridal dress which was quiet heavy. It was a traditional Pakistani-Indian bridal red gown (lehenga) embellished with beautiful golden embroidery and floral patterns. She had her matching fancy embroidered duppata on her head but not wrapped around like a head scarf or a hijab.

They walked through dark streets until they were in an under populated area. The streets were not so wide and uneven with small old houses built in front of each other. There were only two street lights in the whole street out of which one light flickered again and again after some time. The street was abandoned, no one was in it, and it was surrounded by wild trees and hedges. Each house was built keeping a great distance from the other and so there were a lot of trees growing between each house. The tall grass covered the front lawn of mostly every house. They walked across the street a bit more until they were in front of a small white house with trees in its background. This was Khalid's house. Amna was shocked to see what Khalid's house looked like. She thought it was going to be a huge luxury house and she was not wrong to think like that, that's what Rasheed and Khalid had told their house looked like. That's what Amna had been told Khalid's living space looked like so Amna was not wrong to have high expectations of his house. The house was in front of a bunch of trees and surrounded by tall wild grass. Amna could not understand why Khalid had told her lies about his financial situations. She just knew that something was wrong.

While they were standing outside and Khalid was looking for the keys of the main gate of his house, the rest of tho family saw stray dogs walking towards them. Amna was frightened of dogs, she did not hate them but she was scared of them because of some bad experiences she had with a pack of stray dogs as a kid. She started sweating, she asked Khalid to hurry up and when he asked her why she just said, "dogs!" Something slipped from her mother-in-law's mouth that really confused her and made her question actually everything. She said," oh you'll be seeing a lot of those here ,since the door breaks open sometimes, the walk in, you will have to learn to tangle them if you want to live here, also stop acting like a princess, we all know where you came from and how you loved there. It's not a big deal if we told you that we are richer than you, we did not lie, and we only exaggerated it a bit." At this point, Amna was sure that all her family and she were told about the financial state of Khalid was not true. She just hoped that Khalid's family had not lied about Khalid's considerate, humble and friendly personality. Because that was all that she cared about, although her father wanted his daughter to spend her life in the most luxurious way possible just like every other parent hopes for his children, she thought that being loved and cared for was all she needed. She was easy to please, one would think, and this was true since she did not want all the jewels in the world or the most precious treasures, all she needed to be happy was love unlike most people.

Finely before the dogs got to them, Khalid opened the door. Amna was feeling insecure just standing in the middle of an empty, dark street. She picked up her gown and walked through the knee high hay colored wild grass that moved with the blowing winds of the night. The howling wind blowing the dry leafs through the trees around the street blew off Amna's duppata as she held it on her head. They entered the house after Khalid as he turned on the lights. Amna walked into a small room with some sofas sitting at the corners. They all were tired so they went to the sofa and sat down on sofa as Khalid closed the door. Amna was still bewildered, thinking if Khalid was not that rich, how he could have afforded such a lavish and posh marriage hall. And even if he was rich enough, why did he live in a house like this, why did he lie about having a huge house, his own cars, why did his mother say that the exaggerated their financial status; all these questions circled Amna's mind and she started feeling tensed until she thought it would be best to stop thinking negatively.

It was dinner time; Amna knew that Khalid would have arranged something special for their first dinner together. She was really exuberant to see what he and his family had arranged. Her mother in law said, "Amna, you are not going to sit like this all night now are. Go change into something more casual." Amna replied," But mother, it's my first night of marriage, don't you think I should change into something casual right before I go to sleep?" Her mother-in-law said strongly," It's over now! You got married, that's fine, now you're not going to celebrate forever! Go change your dress. And don't call me 'mother', I am not your mother and I will never be and also listen, is this jewelry you're wearing made of gold? Even though your father is too low-paid and destitute to afford gold, yet if it is gold put it in my cupboard, we'll sell it, anyway, what are you going to do with it now, it would be useful to sell it and get some money out of it." Amna thought that her mother in-law had gotten ruder as the wedding had ended. She thought it was very queer for a supposed rich women like her mother-in-law to decide on selling her new daughter-in-law's wedding jewelry. Amna did not want to sell her jewelry, mainly because her father had worked day and night to earn the money to afford it for her; if anything, she thought only he deserved the money that would come from selling the jewelry so she said," Okay, I will go change if that's what you ask. I won't call you mother either if you don't like it. Also I don't want to sell my jewelry right now since I really like it and think we don't need money right now. Anyway, your financial states are pretty stable right now so I don't see a reason for this act." Her mother-in-law got offended and furiously said, "Did you listen what she said! Listen Ms Amna (ironically "respecting" her), I know better than you about what to do and what not to do. Now you are a part of this house, it won't take long to change that so you better start to follow the rules of this house!" Amna was completely shocked to hear these words from a woman who acted and seemed like such a nice and gracious. She was unsure of what to say. She just stood there for a while as there was an awkward silence in the room. She tried to calm her mother-in-law down by saying, "okay, you can do it, I won't mind". Amna went against her will to satisfy her mother-in-law.

She looked over at Nadia who had fallen asleep on the sofa while sitting with Ahtasham and then looked at Khalid and asked, "So, what's there to eat?" Khalid replied, "I asked the Hall management to pack the leftover food and they agreed. I am going to get it from the hall. Now we are not going to let all that foods go to waste, we paid for it." And he walked out the front door. Shabana told her mother that she was going to leave and that her husband was waiting for her in the cab outside. She said good bye to her mother and left without even looking at Amna. Amna felt that she had been ignored but she satisfied herself by telling herself that Shabana must have forgotten to do so. Amna was a girl filled with positive vibes. She never let the negativity of the world get to her and instead spread positivity all around her. She asked her mother-in-law where her room was so that she could change and her mother-in-law had closed her eyes and rested her head against the top edge of the brown sofa back. She just pointed towards a dark room on the opposite corner of the room they were in. Amna was afraid of the dark; she thought to herself, "Well, guess it's time to come over this fear then." She slowly walked towards the small dark room. She did not even know where the switch board was so she could turn on the lights and did not even have a phone to use the torch of. She recited some verses of Qur'an and walked in the room. The light coming from the room outside made it somewhat visible for her to see the Switch board. She thought that her room would be a beautifully decorated room with flower petals everywhere. She smiled and turned on the light. Her smile turned into a frown to see an obnoxious sight of the filthiest room she had seen. From cans of used paint to torn pieces of cloths for window curtains, this room was a complete monstrosity. Cockroaches crawling on the walls, a small flickering light, an old unmade dusty bed and an unwashed floor, all were the worst things she could have imagined for her room of her first night of marriage. For a moment she thought she was dreaming and so she pinched herself to see and turned out, she was not; but she surely wished she was. She was a heavily dressed bride standing in a dirty room; she was unclear of what to do. She thought that her mother-in-law had sent her into the wrong room and so she went to her again and asked, "Are you sure that the room you sent me in is my room because I think there has been a misunderstanding, the room in filthy!" Her mother-in-law told her that it was in fact hers and Khalid's room; she had to clean the room first. Amna was amazed to hear that, nobody told her that she would have to start cleaning like a maid on her first night of her marriage. Amna was not sure of how to react and thought she misheard her mother-in-law. She asked her again and her mother-in-law just rolled her eyes. Amna was new in this house; she was innocent and did not know of what the world could do. She was puzzled and remembered what her father had told her. She had to show her new family that despite being brought up by a single father, she was brought up in a foremost manner. She went to the room and opened up her bag of casual clothes on the dirty bed. She picked one out and started cleaning the room. It took almost an hour for her to just clean the bed, change the bed sheet and mop the floor; the rest was still grimy but it was all she could do in one night.

Everyone was so tired that they did not even get up to talk to the new bride but the new bride herself cleaned her whole room before her husband came. Khalid came back with a pack of food which was barely enough for all of them. Amna woke up her in-laws and served the food. They all dined until, as expected, they realized that the food was not enough. During the dinner, Amna had told Nadia casually about how she cleaned the room; not that she was complaining, but she just wanted to share about her day. Nadia thought that after all the work Amna had done, she deserved to eat more, she was the new bride anyway so Nadia passed her plate to Amna and said, "You can have it, I ate enough at the wedding." Amna smiled and Nadia and took the plate. She would have said no but she was just so hungry, she did not even eat properly at the wedding. Nadia's mother looked at Nadia for giving her food to Amna. There was an eerie silence until Ahtasham broke the ice by asking Khalid about the expanses of the Hall, Khalid replied, "Oh, yeah the hall belongs to one of my friends, I asked him for a loan, I would be paying him the expanses over the course of time. It would be difficult but he is my good friend, he would understand." Then he said something that added to Amna's confusion; he said, "We had to show Amna's family that we were rich, though we aren't." He then giggled before realizing he had said the wrong thing at the wrong time. Everyone especially Amna looked at him with so many questions in her eyes. Amna ate her food and asked her mother-in-law for permission to go to her room. Amna was a well mannered and behaved young lady but her mother-in-law was not used to this attitude and so confusedly she said, "Why are you asking me? Go if you want to go, why you are still annoying me!" Khalid said, "Mother's right, you must know how to behave right in this house. You go to our room; I'll be there in a moment."

Amna decided it would be best to just listen to what Khalid told her to do. She did not say or ask anything about where he was going; she just went to their room. Khalid sat next to his mother and started discussing something in a low voice. Amna was not used to poking her nose into other people's business so she did not pay much attention to what Khalid and his mother were discussing; she just walked away into her room. Amna walked in the room and shut the door behind her as she would usually do. She walked a few steps away from the door to sit on the bed when her mother-in-law yelled from across the room. She vociferated, "Open the door! Why did you close it? I don't know how many times I would have to correct this woman did your father not teach you anything!" Amna did not know what she did wrong; she closed the door because she was that's what anyone would do when they enter their bedroom. She did not understand just why her mother-in-law had yelled so loud and over reacted so much on such a minor issue; although it was not even an issue.

Khalid agreed with his mother and ordered his new wife to open the door instantly. Amna got puzzled and opened the door quickly and stuttered, "What happened mother-in-law? Did I do something wrong?" Her mother-in-law let out a long breath and said, "Amna, It would be really pleasing if you listen to me for once and do what I tell you to!" For some reason, Amna felt that there was an element of presumptuousness in the way her mother-in-law had been speaking to her since the wedding had gotten over but then again, she thought that it was all just in her mind. Amna, anyway, opened the door. She wanted to ask Khalid how long would it take him to come to the room but she decided not to.

She went and sat down cross legged in the middle of the old fashioned wooden framed bed that had a floral patterned cotton bed sheet over it. She had not observed the room carefully earlier. She had some time now so she decided to check out her surroundings a bit. The bedroom was beige colored and seemed to be about ten feet long and ten feet wide. The bed was a double bed with wooden legs in which vines and flowers were carved. The bed was anything but over whelming. There was a window on the left wall of the room which had old pieces of cloths hanging in front of it as window curtains. The blowing winds of the starry night blew the curtains along with it inside the room. The cans of dried up paint were put in the left corner of the room by Amna herself when she cleaned the room. The white paint was peeling off the damp ceiling. On the right wall, just in front of the bed was the old termite infested brown wooden door. The cold laminated stone floor was cold despite the season being mid summers. Maybe it was because of the cold winds that circled the room through the open window. Amna started to feel a little crisp so she decided to get up and shut the window. She turned her head and leaned forward to look out the room to see if Khalid was coming; he was still sitting with his mother which made sense because only a few minutes had passed. She got up and walked bare footed over the cold smooth stone floor. She went up to the window and felt the fresh cold breeze that blew the pleasant smell of the neighboring pine trees along with it. She took a deep breath and looked out to see the back of the house where wild pine trees had grown along with knee high grass. There must have been many wild animals out there; Amna was just sure. Amna leaned out of the window, her hair waved in the blowing air like a fish's fins in water. She looked around to see the rest of the scenario but saw nothing but some trees and a house or two built far apart from each other indulged in darkness of the night. The soothing light of the moon made it visible for her to see the tall waving grass. It felt to Amna as if the land had just been rained over which may have been the reason for the petrichor in the air. She pulled her head back in and closed the window. She then walked to her bed and sat down again. She looked out the door to see Khalid but she couldn't. She assumed he was in the washroom or in some other room and so she waited for him patiently. She waited for him for almost an hour before her body fell back on the bed as she fell asleep.

CHAPTER FOUR

The next morning, Amna woke up expecting Khalid to be by her side nut to her surprise, he was not. She got muddled and so got up to go see where he was. Amna was habitual of waking up early so despite being tired from last day, it was around seven in the morning when she woke up. She went to the only washroom in the house to perform ablution for her Fajar prayer. Amna was really religious and was used to praying five times a day. She went to the stuffy, steamy washroom and almost slipped over the old broken tiled floor before gaining control again. After offering her prayer, she went to the kitchen to get something to eat. She saw that her mother-in-law was in the kitchen, waiting for her to come. Amna was only curious about one thing and that was "where is Khalid?" She decided to ask his mother about where he was. Amna's mother-in-law hesitated for a moment ant then told her that he went to work LAST NIGHT. She further told Amna that he would be going to the main city on a weekly basis as his workplace is there. This took Amna by surprise. She was not told about any of this, rather she was lied to about most of the things. Amna understood the situation because she knew how difficult it was to earn money, especially when there is only one person earning for the whole family, it is difficult to afford certain expanses. Amna still thought that it would have been pleasing if Khalid had taken at least a week off work but expressing her opinion just made the situation worse as her mother-in-law started snubbing her for not being corporative. Out of curiosity, Amna asked her mother-in-law about the subject of their hour long discussion last night. To that, her mother-in-law said, "Stop interfering between me and my son, just because you are married to him, doesn't mean I can't talk to him privately. Don't poke your nose into our business." Amna stayed quiet and apologized for no reason; thinking it would calm her mother-in-law down.

Amna's mother-in-law was in the kitchen and so Amna immediately went up to her and said, "You don't have to work, I will prepare breakfast for everyone." Amna was expecting her mother-in-law to smile or maybe praise her but instead she rudely said, "Of course YOU are going to prepare the breakfast; who will do it otherwise. It's your duty from now on, you have to do all the house chores from now on." Amna was not too quick at judging people but now her mother-in-law was not even tired or anything, Amna realized she was just rude sometimes or maybe that was the way she talked to everyone.

Amna, at this point was actually a tad bit annoyed about most of the things but mostly for Khalid not being here with her on the first day of her marriage. Amna was always regarded for what she did as an unmarried girl at her father's house by her father so when she saw that no one especially her mother-in-law praised her for what she did, it really demotivated her. The amount of chores that had to be done in that house was not that easy to complete, especially by a seventeen year old girl. She was still destined to do all that by herself just to satisfy and somehow impress her mother-in-law. Amna used to do a lot of house chores at her father's house including doing the dishes, washing the cloths and cleaning the house in general but because Khalid's house was a little bigger than Amna's and also because she did not have anyone else with her who would help her in completing her tasks, it was difficult for her to do so; yet she did not complain.

Anyway, Amna started to prepare breakfast for the family. She made omelets, roties/flat breads and tea for everyone. Of course she had a good experience in doing so since she had been doing this since she was a little kid. Everyone loved the breakfast except of course her mother-in-law who thought that the omelet was too salty and the tea was too sweet for her. Anyway, everyone else loved it so it was an achievement for Amna but she still wanted to satisfy her mother-in-law so she kept on trying harder and harder to cook better and follow each and everything that her mother-in-law said but alas, nothing that Amna did made the old grumpy woman happy.

That very day, Khalid's eldest brother Rasheed came to visit with his wife. This was the same person who came to ask for Amna's hand in marriage for his brother and told all those white lies. He was still not hesitant and did not feel guilty to face Amna despite knowing the fact that Amna would have already caught all the lies he told her. Rasheed did not care what anyone thought of him, he just did what he wanted to. He had married the woman of his choice despite the disapproval of his own mother. He loved his wife dearly and did not bare a wrong word about her. His mother still loved him from the depths of her heart unlike Khalid, whom she loved superficially. Rasheed bought Shabana along with him just so the whole family would sit together and enjoy; at least that's what he hoped he would do.

It was around 02:00 pm when they arrived so Amna felt it was perfect time to serve tea with some cookies she had made earlier. She asked everyone if they would drink tea. Everyone except Shabana asked for a warm cup of tea. (In this text, the tea being referred to is the British milk tea). Amna went to the kitchen and prepared tea for four people. Everyone was sitting in the main living room which was the first room when entering the house. Shabana meanwhile, got up to check on Amna. Amna was done with the tea. She put some cookies in a dish and put it in a tray along with four cups of hot steaming tea. She was walking out the kitchen when she came across Shabana. Amna said, "If you needed anything, you could've asked me for it, do you need anything?" Shabana rolled her eyes as usual and said harshly, "This is my house, I can do whatever I want; if I need something, I can get it myself. And by the way, why are there four cups of tea, aren't there only three people to serve?" Amna replied, "One is for mother-in-law, one is for Mr.Rasheed, one for Mrs. Rasheed and one is for me." Shabana giggled; confused, Amna looked at Shabana. For some reason, even unknown to Amna herself, she could see flames of hatred burning in Shabana's eyes. Making fun of Amna she said, "Know your place, who allowed you to make tea for yourself! Give that to me." And then took a cup off the tray as she walked towards the living room. Amna for a moment stood there, puzzled to as what had just happened. She was really confused to see how her in-laws except Nadia and Ahtasham had changed their behavior negatively right after the marriage.

Amna went to the living room where the guests were and served the tray of tea and cookies in front of them on the wooden table. Rasheed's wife was not scared to say anything or to express her opinion mainly because she knew that her husband loved her and protected her at all costs. She took a bite off one of the cookies and took a sip of tea to wash it down. She told everyone that the cookies were delectable and asked about their baker. Amna proudly said that she had baked the cookies earlier that day. Rasheed took a bite off one cookie and agreed with his wife. As expected by Amna, her mother-in-law ate a whole cookie and still thought it was not good but Rasheed opposed her opinion mainly because that was not what his wife thought. Shabana came into the room and sat down with them as they all continued talking about their day.

Rasheed asked his mother about Khalid and where he was. She told him that he was off to work. Rasheed frowned for a moment in confusion and said, "Did he not take some days off work?" His mother said, "Oh you know, he has to work to run this house. We had no choice." Rasheed then told that he took three months off work after his marriage but still thought that Khalid not taking even a day off work was perfectly fine, keeping in mind the situation.

Perhaps the situation he was not noticing was that Khalid had married and bought home a seventeen year old girl away from her family and was not even giving her enough time. Rasheed's wife did not speak much but he understood each and every unspoken word of hers. Amna really loved their couple and admired the love they had for each other. She thought for a moment and then said what she thought. This caused her mother-in-law to get offended as she thought that girls were supposed to be shy and were not supposed to say things like that. Rasheed and his wife however, were really opened minded and so loved the compliment and enjoyed it. They kept on talking for hours and hours before, of course, it was time for them to leave. Rasheed's mother asked him to spend the night at her house but Rasheed's wife did not agree so they left. Shabana went with them.

The day passed by until it was night. Nadia and Ahtasham had been to school all day and they had just come back. They all decided to play a board game called ludo. The board game was lying around for a while and they were bored and so they thought it be great to play a game with the new family member. They started playing the game forming teams. Because there were only three people, one team of two was formed while Nadia wanted to play as an individual. Amna asked Nadia if she wanted to team up with her but Nadia thought it would improve her skills if she played as an individual. Obviously, Amna's mother-in-law did not like Amna playing despite knowing the fact that Amna was young and had a keen desire to enjoy. She continuously asked Amna to stop playing and do something for her but after Amna did what her mother-in-law told her to, she continued the game. They were having an amazing time except for Amna's mother-in-law. It seemed like Amna and Ahtasham were winning. Nadia did not get frustrated because she was losing. Amna got really involved in the game. Amna convinced herself that this was her own family but for the first time, it actually felt like it was.

There was a knock at the door. Amna's mother-in-law asked her to go ask who was it and open the door. They stopped the game so that Amna could go. She asked who it was and to her delight, it was Khalid. She got really enthusiastic and opened the door instantly. She greeted him and asked him to come in as she took his suitcase and hung his coat. Khalid did not greet Amna the way she was hoping to be greeted but then again she blamed it all on his tiredness. She asked Nadia and Ahtasham to wait a little longer as she prepared the tea for Khalid. She prepared the tea and served it to Khalid and his mother. Khalid and his mother were sitting on the couch in the same room where Amna, Ahtasham and Nadia were playing Ludo. Khalid talked to his mother as they both watched Amna play with Nadia and Ahtasham. Amna felt wired that even though she is the new family member and the wife of Khalid and he has seen her for the second time after marriage, he was not excited to talk to her. Rather whispered to his mother. Amna did not know that her husband was whispering to his mother about how much he hated when Amna got along with Ahtasham. Ahtasham was much more stunning than Khalid and also Amna's age fellow so it was no wonder why Khalid was insecure about Amna developing feelings for his brother. Amna thought of Ahtasham as her brother and Nadia as her sister. She had no feelings for Ahtasham except the ones a sister has for her brother. She was sincere to Khalid and loved him and so she could have never cheated on Khalid with anyone else. Amna did not let another negative thought about what Khalid was whispering about and why was he whispering come too her mind and she sat down on the ground to continue the game.

The game ended and Ahtasham and Amna won. Nadia still was not frustrated because she knew that it was just a fun game. Khalid had a grin on his face as stared at Amna and then at Ahtasham. Amna had not noticed that as Amna and Ahtasham high-fived in joy. Khalid got furious but he did not say a word. He stood up from his place on the couch aggressively as his mother watched him and stomped off to his bedroom. This turned Amna's joyous moment to a worrisome and confused moment in time. She did not know what happened but still her heart was pounding. He mother-in-law frowned at her as she said, "I do not understand why this woman has no manners! Did you father not teach you anything? You stupid girl! Look what you did, he had come from work, exhausted and you made him furious. Who asked you to get so casual with Ahtasham, you're a girl, stay in your limits or I know very well how to make you stay in your limits."

She said this and then mumbled something angrily before going out of the living room and into Khalid's bedroom.

This was the first time Amna's eyes filled with tears. Nadia noticed tears filling up in her hazel eyes filled up with tears and a drop of tears rolled down her rose red cheek. Nadia quickly crawled towards Amna and hugged her. Amna did not utter a word, tears rolled down her eyes as she shut her eyes tightly. Ahtasham felt guilty because he knew very well that Khalid did all this because he was with Nadia. Instead of fighting for the right, he walked out of the house because he knew that if he said a single word in favor of Amna, Khalid's doubt would turn into a fact in his mind. Amna sniveled while in the arms of Nadia. She was confused and heartbroken so it made sense for her to shed a tear in distress. Amna had never thought of staying away from her family, mainly her father but the only reason she agreed to do so was because Khalid and his family loved her so much that she thought she would feel just at home at Khalid's house as well but that certainly was not the case. First, Amna thought Shabana and her mother-in-law acted rude on the day of her marriage because they were tired, then she assumed that her mother-in-law just talked to everyone like that; she did not care much about how Shabana talked to her because she knew that Shabana was married and she was not

going to be with Amna all the time. She did not care about a thing because she knew Khalid loved her, he said he loved her; she thought he loved her...

Months went by and heartbreaking incidents like this became a routine for Amna but she still got hurt by each one of them like it was the very first time. Nadia was the only one who consoled Amna in her harsh times. Amna wanted to study just like Nadia did and that was what they had promised her and her father but that promise never became a reality. Even Ahtasham stepped back after he felt that his presence with Amna was causing a lot of trouble. Nadia was still there, trusting, consoling and protecting Amna like a sister and a real friend.

It seemed like troubles came to stay at this house uninvited until...

CHAPTER FIVE

Happiness and bliss knocked at the family's door. They had their first baby; a baby boy they named 'Hamza'. The cutest little baby boy they had ever seen. With his golden brown hair, umber colored eyes, rose red cheeks, adorable small pink lips, he was an angel. He was, in fact, one of the very few people who could melt Amna's mother-in-law's heart. She absolutely adored him mainly because he was her son's first ever child. She had become a grandmother for the first time; it was no doubt that she felt it a magical moment for her. Khalid loved him from the depths of his heart.

Everyone treasured and adored the new little family member except for Shabana. She absolutely hated him for the sole reason that he was Amna's son. Because she hated Amna, she ultimately hated her son, Hamza as well. Hamza was the reason Amna's mother-in-law started to love her a little bit, just a little bit but it was enough for Amna. Hamza also bought some love for Amna in Khalid's heart and he started to care for her. Amna was really happy and just to add to her enchantment, her mother-in-law allowed her to use the phone to call her family and ask them to come visit her. Amna was on cloud nine. She did not have the permission to use the phone or call her family so this was an exciting moment for her. As soon as she got her mother-in-laws permission to call her family, she literally ran to the telephone and started to dial her father's telephone number.

Her speed as well as her enthusiasm faded when she realized that her father was living under the delusion that his daughter was living in a huge luxurious house with people who loved her dearly. She stopped for a moment and thought about how much it would hurt her father to see where and how she was living; all she cared about was her father's joy. She then thought to herself, "Maybe they (her in-laws) would act nice in front of father, and maybe, just maybe he won't mind me living in this kind of house." But she knew pretty well that realizing that all that Rasheed said were lies would hurt him a lot. For then, she knew he would be too happy for her and her son to notice anything else so she continued dialing his number.

She waited for him to pick up the phone and as soon as he did, she enthusiastically asked if it was her father on the other side of the phone as she exclaimed, "hello, Father?"Her father closed his eyes as a tear of joy rolled down his eyes to hear his most beloved daughter's voice after almost a year. Amna again asked, "Hello, are you there Papa?" He did not say anything; he just enjoyed the voice of his daughter which sounded like the best music to his ears. After a while, he replied, "Yes my dearest, sweetest daughter. Yes I am here my darling.", as another streak of tears rolled down his wrinkled face. Amna felt a sudden shock of joy and satisfaction to hear her father's voice.

She smiled as she took a deep break and said with bliss, "Father, you are a grandfather now." Her father laughed with joy and got really excited to meet her. She invited him over to her house over the phone. He was really excited to see his days-old grandson and could not wait to visit her. He asked if he could bring Haya and Shazia along with him and Amna said he could bring everyone from the family along with him, there was no problem at all. He was so excited that he put the receiver of the telephone down and addressed Haya who lived with her father and told her about everything. She jumped and laughed with joy as her father told her to pack her cloths because they were going to leave to get to Khalid's house tomorrow. It was a beautiful moment filled with ecstasy.

The next day, early in the morning when everyone had just woke up, Amna's family arrived. Amna's mother-in-law was completely aware that they were going to come and so she did not cause any trouble. Shabana did come to see the new baby but left before the night ended to go to her house. On the phone with Khalid, Amna's father asked for the directions to his house. When he came to the location Khalid had told him to come to, he was shocked and surprised. This was not what he was expecting to see. As Amna had imagined earlier, he got puzzled and asked Khalid about what was going on. Khalid knew he and his family were in trouble because of all those white lies they had told. He hesitantly asked Amna's father to come inside his house to talk. Her father agreed and walked in the house with Haya and Shazia carrying a bag of cloths. They sat down on the couch putting the bag of cloths next to them on the floor.

Amna asked to make tea as she usually did but her father stopped her and surprised, he said, "Why would you work in the kitchen in this condition, sit down. Khalid don't you stop her from doing work?" To that, Khalid's mother nicely replied, "Amna, have we ever asked you to do work before? Why are you going to do it now? Now look, your father thinks that were so cruel that we make you do all the house chores." She then ordered Nadia to make tea for all the people.

Amna's father questioned Khalid about their house and why had they lied to him. Khalid did not know what to say and so he came up with another lie. He told him that they did not lie about their financial states at all. In fact, they had faced a terrible tragedy due to which their financial states had been negatively impacted. He told him that his partner in business had betrayed him and taken over his business. He told Amna's father that because of this, they had to sell their lavish house and shift to this house. He solidified his point by saying, "If I were not rich, how would I have been able to afford that luxurious marriage hall?" what Amna's family did not know was that he had taken loans to afford a day in that marriage hall. He further played the victim by saying, "It's a cruel world out there." The story he came up with was a bad excuse but the way he told it made everyone believe it. For a moment, even Amna felt convinced about all what her husband said but she just came to know one thing by the way Khalid lied; he was a great liar. Because Amna had witnessed a moment or two where Khalid had lied with excellence, she realized it would be best for her not to trust everything he would say in the future until she herself would see it with her eyes.

Nadia prepared the tea for everyone while Amna, for the first time sat with the guests and as she had hoped, her in-laws were unbelievably nice to her in front of her father. Haya was really excited to meet her sister, Amna after such a long time. She did not hold back from getting up from her place and sitting with Amna to talk to her and just her. She talked to Amna so much that Amna could not even talk to anyone else, even her own father. After all, she had a lot to say to her sister.

Her father was quite impatient at this point. He wanted to see what his grandson looked like and so he asked Amna to bring Hamza to him. She nodded as she got up and went to her room to get Hamza. Hamza was put on Amna's bed, wrapped in a fuzzy pastel blue blanket. His chubby angelic face was wrapped in the blanket as he slept. Amna looked at him and smiled with delight. She moved towards him and very carefully and slowly, picked him up in her arms. She stayed very quiet trying not to wake up the new born baby. She then walked out of the room and to her father.

Her father's eyes gleamed with bliss and excitement to see his grandson. He spread out his arms towards Amna and asked her to hand him the child. She slowly leaned towards her father and put Hamza in his arms. Amna's father could not contain his excitement. He was beyond delighted. He looked at Hamza's angelic face and said, "He is just like you Amna, when you were a baby. It feels like I am carrying you as a baby in my arms. I can see it; the same almond shaped eyes and the small nose and pouty pink lips. He is just like you!"

Haya was really enthusiastic to hold the baby in her arms as well; after all, it was her sister's first child. Despite Shazia being the oldest of the sisters and being married as well, she did not have any children yet. She just never wanted to have children but when she saw the captivating beauty of Amna's baby, she changed her mind. She smiled and asked her father if she could hold the baby in her arms for a while but he was captivated by his grandson like a firework show. After Shazia repeated herself several times, her father finely heard her and put the baby in his daughter's arm who was sitting just next to him. Shazia did not say anything, she just grinned at the baby for a while; holding him close to her face. Haya could not hold herself back no matter how hard she tried to. She started to ask Shazia to give her Hamza until the point where Shazia and in fact, everyone got annoyed. She finely got Hamza in her arms and it felt to her like she had accomplished every goal in life. She hugged the baby and held him close to herself.

Haya did not know how to handle babies very well and so even though she did not want to but she made Hamza wake up. As soon as he woke up, he felt like he was in someone else's arms other than his mother's, he started to cry. Haya got confused and started to talk in a baby voice as she made silly faces to make Hamza calm again but he did not sit quiet until he was in the arms of his mother, whom he thought of as his only protection. Everyone laughed genuinely to see Haya act goofy except for Amna's in-laws who just faked a smile.

Amna was really happy to meet her family after such a long time and the fact that she was now a mother just added to her joy. Amna's brother, Tahir had not come along with his family. He instead stayed at home because he had to go to work. Amna's father asked her if they could stay for just that night. Amna did not answer; instead she just looked at her mother-in-law to see what she wanted. Her mother-in-law happily said, "Well, of course you can, think of this house as your own!" Amna's family felt very welcomed to hear that. Amna tried not to get too excited about how her in-laws were acting so nice to everyone because she knew that it was just a matter of time before they showed into their original behavior. Amna knew that all the kindness and humble attitude that her mother-in-law was showing was going to go away as soon as her family leaves the house so she thought to herself, "Well, guess I should enjoy it while it lasts."

Amna thought as a human, it was her right to speak up for herself to her only support, her father but then again as a mother and a considerate daughter, she only thought of two thing; "What would happen to Hamza if I tell my father the truth and possibly split up with Khalid?" and "People would taunt me and my father for all our lives if I break up with Khalid." She was not wrong to think that, the society likes to point out other's flaws while completely ignoring their beauty. Amna thought that because her sisters were staying with her all night, they had the whole night to themselves just to talk. With Amna's great excitement for the night came her fear of her saying something that might upset her father that night.

The balmy evening passed and it was time for dinner. Amna's mother-in-law knew that there was nothing to cook in the house but still wanted put a good impression on Amna's family so she did not say anything. Khalid did not have enough money to buy anything from the market. While Khalid and his mother were in the kitchen, discussing the matter, Nadia, Ahtasham, Amna and her sisters and father were sitting in the living room talking. Nadia was quiet talkative, just like Haya and so she did not think much before she spoke. Despite her mother strictly forbidding her from saying that there is not food in the house in front of Amna's family, she still said it and instantly regretted it as well. There was a silence in the room as everyone stopped talking and, for a moment, thought of what slipped Nadia's mouth. Amna's father heard this and felt bad for Khalid and his family since he believed what Khalid had said earlier about his partner betraying him in business.

He thought that for a family that was once so rich to suddenly turn poor must have been really difficult and so he pulled out his wallet, opened it and saw a total of two hundred rupees in his old worn out, brown faux leather wallet. He pulled the money out and called Khalid in to the living room. In the kitchen, Khalid and his mother were busy finding a solution to the problem when Khalid and his mother heard Amna's father. Khalid's mother annoyingly said, "What's the problem with that man now!"

Khalid walked in the room and saw the money

in his father-in-law's hands. He moved further towards him and asked if he needed something. Amna's father spread his arm forward and asked him to take the money. Khalid told him that he did not need the money and acted as if he was extremely hesitant to take the money though deep down inside, he just wanted one person to ask him to take the money again and he would have snatched the money.

They were having this conversation when his mother walked in and saw Amna's father giving Khalid the money. She got really happy and excited but did not let that come to her face and instead just went up to Amna's father and said, "You really don't have to." Amna's father insisted again because he thought that they were hesitant because they had never taken money from someone before because they were really affluent. Khalid's mother said, "Well, Khalid if he is insisting so much, you can accept it and go get something to eat for everyone. Khalid quickly took the money from his father-in-law's hands and walked out the main gate after telling everyone that he was going to get food. Despite Amna's father being needier than Khalid's family, he still had an open-hand and was really generous towards everyone from an unknown beggar to one of his family members.

Khalid came back with a plastic bag in his hand which contained flat breads and curry. He had some money with him as well and he also took his father-in-law's money so Amna had thought that he would have brought amazing food but as soon as she opened the package, she was indeed shocked. There was some curry which was not even enough for four people and eight flat breads to eat with the curry. Nadia served the dinner and as expected, the food was not enough but Amna's family did not complain about a single thing. Amna knew that Khalid had bought cheap food just so he could keep some money to himself. This annoyed Amna but she held herself back from saying anything mainly because she did not like causing trouble.

Dinner was over and so Nadia, Amna and her sisters went to Nadia's room to spend the night talking. Unfortunately, Nadia's room and her mother's room were side by side so they all agreed to speak in a very low voice. Amna's father was also present there with them. Khalid and his mother had gone to bed but Amna, Amna's family and Nadia were still up, having a joyous time talking and laughing until Amna's mother-in-law opened the door to the room with a grin on her face. Everyone stopped talking and looked at her as she said in a fit of pique, "That's enough talking for one night; go to bed now, all of you. Amna you go to your room and I have put a mattress down on the living room floor, your family can sleep there, I have put blankets there as well." Amna's mother-in-law walked out, slamming the door behind her. Amna said good night to everyone as she asked her father to come outside the room for a while as she had to talk about something important. Her father knew what she was going to say and so had already prepared an answer.

She said, "Did you see that father? This is how everyone talks to me in this house. I have cried several times but no one values my tears of distress. I don't want to stay here anymore, they all lied to us." Her father in reply, very calmly said, "Amna, remember what I told you on the day we left; always remember that. I know that they lied but sometimes you have to adjust when you get married. Getting separated will never be an option and should never be an option for you, my daughter. Always remember my teaching. Try to change them, don't let them change you. Be the drop of ink and let them be the water; now that you have been dropped in the water, mix up with the water but color the water with your pigment as well." Amna nodded with a heavy heart because she thought that all her father was doing was just telling her to let her in-laws do whatever they wanted to her but she was a little too young to understand what her father told her.

CHAPTER SIX

The next morning, they all woke up at the dusk. Amna's family had to go to their house. Her mother-in-law acted as if she did not want them to leave but the way she was talking, it was clear to any intelligent person that Amna's mother-in-law did not want Amna's family to stay at her house anymore though it had only been a night but she was already fed up with them. Nadia asked her mother to take her day off school so that she could say her good bye to Amna's family but her mother thought that it was senseless to skip school for such a minor reason.

Anyway, Nadia prepared breakfast for everyone including herself and served it. Before she went to school, she made sure she warmly said her good bye to everyone. A moment after Nadia and Ahtasham left for school, Amna's family decided to leave as well. They did not want to waste any time because Amna's father had to go to work. They left the house and Amna knew that all her in-laws were about to change so she braced herself for the impact.

As soon as her family left, her mother-in-law's usual grin came back to her face. Khalid asked for his mother's permission to leave for work and as soon as his mother said yes, he left; without even saying good bye to Amna. Amna was very sentimental, her eyes filled with tears about the smallest of the situations but after she had seen what was happening in her new home, she tried to strengthen up a bit; but of course, it was not possible to do so in such little time.

When she saw the way Khalid ignored her, she just stood there, with tears in her eyes; she said nothing as teardrops rolled down her cheeks. Her mother-in-law looked at her, rolled her eyes and walked in the house leaving her all alone outside to cry. Amna let out a breath as she could no longer hold herself back and started to cry. She knew this was going to happen and so was not shocked at all, she was just distressed. She just got too used to her father's and sisters' love all over again. This time not even Nadia was there to console her. She cried standing all alone, outside the house in an empty street as the tall wild grass hid half of her legs and the wind blew her hair with it like an egret set free after a long time.

After a while, she was over the matter and finely had stopped crying. She took in a deep breath of the fresh morning gale and let it out with all her despondency and sadness. She wiped her tears with her sleeves and decided to go inside. She turned around to open the door hoping her mother-in-law would have left it open for her but she was wrong. The door was locked from the inside. She pulled the door using the door handle thinking it was just stuck but after she pulled it with all her force for a couple of times, she got sure that the door was locked.

She knocked on the door once…twice…thrice; but there was no response. Inside, her mother-in-law heard the knocks but she did not bother opening the door for her daughter-in-law. She just liked teasing her daughter-in-law and she was really good at it as well. Amna knocked on the door harder thinking no one heard the knock the first time but all in vein. At this point, she got sure that her mother-in-law was not opening the door despite hearing the knocks on purpose.

She turned around and sat down cross-legged on the foot mat lying in front of the main door. She threw her head down in despair as she uncontrollably shed a tear. Her mother-in-law cared so less about her that she, after locking Amna out, got busy in her own work. When she heard such strong knocks on the door, she was in fact, shocked. She thought that Amna's father had returned for some reason and had seen Amna outside and he was the one who knocked so hard. She got frightened as to what was going to happen. With trembling legs, she got up and in a shivering voice, she asked, "Who is it?" On hearing no reply, Amna's mother-in-law got even more frightened. She opened the door and actually, got shocked to see only Amna standing in front of her. She was actually expecting her father with her for some reason. She took a deep breath of comfort and thanked god that her father did not see the way she treated his daughter. She then angrily asked Amna why she was knocking the door so hard. Amna did not reply, instead she pushed her mother-in-law back, stepped instead walked straight to her room where Hamza was.

Her mother in law got furious to see Amna's behavior. She followed Amna into her room but could not get to her because Amna locked the door just before her mother-in-law entered it. Her mother-in-law threatened her that if she would not open the door before she counted to three, she was going to call Khalid. She thought that Amna was going to get scared and open the door but Amna was wise, she knew that by law, even if she got divorced, Hamza was going to stay with her and her mother-in-law did not want that at all. Amna did not bother to reply and stayed quiet. She just said, "Go ahead! Get me divorced, Hamza is going to stay with me anyway and that is all I care about." Her mother-in-law thought of what Amna said for a while. It was not long before she realized that she was going to make a big mistake. Her mother-in-law then tried to make her open the door by acting nice but Amna knew that it was all a part of her plan to get Hamza. Her mother-in-law thought that as soon as Amna was going to open the door, she was going to take Hamza away from Amna and lock her in.

In a while, the telephone lying on the three legged brown wooden table put next to the couch rang. Amna's mother-in-law approached the phone and picked the receiver up. It was her daughter, Samina, on the other side of the line. Amna's mother-in-law asked her why she called and she started by reminding her how she was expecting a baby. She further told her that she and her husband had just had a baby boy. This news made her mother genuinely delighted and happy. She told her daughter that she was going to come to her house in a moment as she put the receiver down enthusiastically. She indirectly told Amna that she was going out of the house but did not bother to mansion why or where she was going. She wore her chador and quickly walked out the house slamming the door behind her. Despite knowing the fact that there was not food for her or Hamza in the house, she made sure to lock the door of the house from the outside so that Amna could not go anywhere; even out to get food.

Amna waited for her mother-in-law to leave and as soon as she heard the main door slam shut, she unlocked her bedroom door and walked out; keeping an open eye for her mother-in-law. She feared that her mother-in-law was still doing this to get Hamza away from her. She poked her head out of her room and looked left and right to see if her mother-in-law was out there, hiding. She was holding Hamza tightly in her arms so that her mother-in-law could not snatch him from her. She took a sigh of relief as she finely was confirmed that her mother-in-law was no longer in the house.

Amna was still curious to know where her mother-in-law had gone. While she was thinking of possible place she could have gone to, Hamza started to cry. As a mother, she knew the reason for his crying; he was hungry. She decided to go to the kitchen and get something to eat for her son. When she entered the kitchen, she saw that there was absolutely no food in the house. She checked the cabinets, the refrigerator-everywhere but still could not find any food. As a person who plans for the future, she had some packs of baby food in her purse which was hidden in her closet. She quickly filled Hamza's baby feeder with warm water and rushed to her room to get the packs of baby food. She prepared the baby food for him and fed him half of it, saving half for later use. She was not really hungry because she had just eaten breakfast.

After this, she continued thinking where her mother-in-law could have possibly gone to. She then remembered that before her mother-in-law left, she received a telephone call from someone. Usually Amna was never interested in what other people were doing, she let them do what they wanted to but this time, she was just really curious to get all her desired answers. She put Hamza on the couch and luckily, the telephone was set on auto-record which meant that it recorded each and every call. She listened to the most recent call and came to know why her mother-in-law was so hyped. She actually, herself got quite excited to hear the news, in fact she wanted to see the little baby boy as soon as she could. She was happy that Hamza was going to have a cousin his age when he grows up.

Despite being a woman herself, her mother-in-law strongly believed that males were superior to females for several of her own made up reasons. This meant that if someone had a child and it was a boy, that person especially the mother, was going to be cared for and respected whereas on the other hand if someone had a baby girl, that person mostly the mother was going to get taunted and treated badly by everyone to the point where one would expect the mother to break down. Her mother-in-law was beyond enchanted, first her son had a baby boy and then her daughter had a son; it was like her dreams came true.

CHAPTER SEVEN

A few troubled years passed for Amna but still these troubles were not even the fraction of the troubles she was going to face in her life. She was still in comfort because of Hamza. Hamza was now six. Samina's son was a few months younger to Hamza. They both were almost age fellows and so were great friends. They used to play together all day long before they had to go to sleep. Despite Samina living in another house, her son used to stay at her mother's house because Samina and her husband; both had to go to work. Hamza and Samina's son went to separate schools; Samina's son went to a muck expensive and better school whereas Hamza went to a much low standard school but they still were best friends.

Amna loved their friendship and completely adored it. This was not the case with Samina; she completely hated Hamza because he was Amna's son but Amna loved Samina's son because he was just a kid and despite that, Amna never had any harsh feeling for her sister-in-law unlike Samina. Samina's son used to share all his food with Hamza which used to infuriate Samina because she thought that the food she fed her son was 'too expensive and lavish' to be shared with someone of such a lower class such as Hamza. She thought he did not deserve to eat that which her son ate but children's hearts are free of hatred or the concept of poverty or affluence and so Samina's son could not understand what his mother said. Actually, Samina was being childish while her child unknowingly acted like an adult. Despite her hatred for Amna, Samina's mother-in-law did not mind the two boys playing together because they were both her grandsons and that's what she wanted; all of her grand children to be males. When Samina saw that despite her restricting Amna from letting Hamza play with her son, there was still no change; she thought it was time to do something by her. What could have Amna done, she did want to force her child to stay away from his best friend.

Samina was furious and wanted to take her son away from Hamza's 'bad influence' as soon as she could. She came up with a plan and thought it was genius. She planed that she was going to put some money from her mother's cabinet into Amna's and blame Hamza for stealing money for his mother. It was an awful plan but she knew that her mother would believe anything that is against Amna and Khalid would always believe her mother. As planned, she quietly went to her mother's room, took some money from the lower cabinet and put it in Amna's cabinet.

It did not take a while for her mother to realize that some money was missing from her cabinet; there was not much money to keep track of anyway. She was over dramatic and always caused a lot of tension for little problem. She shouted as she called her daughter, Samina into her room and asked her about the money. Samina, obviously, 'had no idea where it was' but something she did know was that she had seen Amna's son come into the room earlier. Her mother thought that she was talking without thinking of what she was saying. "What could that little boy have done" she cried as she continued searching for the money in her cabinet. Samina said, "I am not saying Hamza has done it, I am just saying that someone might have made him do it." This put her mother in doubt. Her first target was Amna. She angrily asked her if she had stolen the money or made her son steal the money. She said no because she had not done such a thing. Her mother-in-law however did not trust her and so, she grasped Amna by her arm and pulled her with herself as she darted towards Amna's bedroom. She called Samina along with her to be a witness. Of course Samina 'had a feeling' that the money was with Amna. Amna's mother-in-law threw Amna on the bed as she turned and opened the cabinet. At first, she did not see anything but then because her doubt was getting stronger, she started to throw Amna's things out of the wooden cabinet. All of Amna's old pictures and Polaroid of her family fell on the ground in front of her eyes as Samina carelessly stepped on them.

Not too long had passed and finely, her mother-in-law found what she was looking for. Samina smiled to see the money; the smile she passed because she knew what was coming for Amna. Samina's mother let out a sigh of relief as she held the money in her hands right before she turned and faced Amna. Amna was surprised to see the money in her mother-in-law's hands. She was confused and did not know how the money had gotten there when she had not put it in her cabinet.

Amna's mother-in-law furiously asked Amna why she had stolen the money. Amna was confused, she innocently said, "I did not!" Samina favored her mother by saying, "Then how did it get in your cabinet? Oh maybe you made Hamza steal it. Mother, I am telling you, if you want your grandson to not become a liar and a thief whom Amna is making him, keep him away from her." Samina's mother thought for a short while and then slowly said, "Your right! I must keep my grandson away from her to protect him." Amna looked at them both and got back on her feet and said, "Hamza did not do it, and neither did I! You can't take my son away from me." Neither Samina nor her mother said anything; they just walked out of the room. Amna followed them but before she could get out, Samina locked the door from the outside. Amna hit the door hard with her palm as she cried, "You can't do this to me! He is my son. Don't take my son away from me, I beg you!" She tried to punk the door to open it but her knuckles started to bleed. She continued kicking and hitting the door in hopes someone would open it; maybe she still could not guess what kind of people her in-laws were. After several failed attempts to get the door to open, Amna sat down on the cold hard floor and started to cry uncontrollably. She ran her fingers through her hair as she sobbed until she passed out.

On the roof, Samina was taking cloths off the line when she saw that her son and Hamza were still playing together. Her blood boiled to see this. She thought of teaching Amna and her son a final lesson. She darted towards Hamza and grasped him by his wrist as she asked her son to go get water for her. As soon as her son went down the stairs, she started to drag Hamza to the edge of the borderless roof. Hamza never saw what was coming for him next. For a moment, it seemed to Samina as if time had stopped as she felt guilty and asked herself, "Should I do this?" But then she continued to drag a young woman's first child to the dangerous edge of the hard concrete roof. Hamza said, "Please let me go aunt, my wrist hurts." She replied, "Don't worry, all our pains will end soon." She thought to herself, "This may not be the right thing to do but it sure is the only way to teach Amna a lesson!" as she looked down the roof of the house. At this point, Hamza had started to try to get free from Samina's hold. Samina did not give her decision another thought and threw the little boy off the roof and watched him fall to his death as he screamed his mother's name for help on the top of his lungs.

As soon as he hit the ground, Samina started to scream and act as if he had fallen by accident and thought that she was going to tell everyone that he slipped by himself. Downstairs, her mother also got attentive and got curious to know what caused such a loud noise. Nadia had just come home from school; she also rushed outside to see what had happened. Samina dashed down the stairs to make it seem like she really cared and then joined her mother and sister as they all walked out. Inside Amna's room, she had woken up to the noise outside. She got up from the cold floor and stood up. She asked what had happened but heard no replies. She got concerned. Nadia and her mother asked Samina what had happened and she just said, "Hamza fell!" This caused her mother to lose her mind and rush outside. She made it seem like she really cared and loved Hamza. It is a fact, universally acknowledged, if a person does not love another person's parents, he is not going to love the other person as well. Nadia was the first to step out the main door and see the body of a six year old boy lying on the ground surrounded by grass covered in blood. Nadia screamed to see such a sight.

Nadia's mother did not feel such intense emotions as she should have felt. She herself had thought that she was not going to be able to see him in pain but actually it was for some reason fine for her. She was sad but just sad. Nadia rushed back in and began to open the old fashioned lock on Amna's bedroom. Amna continuously worriedly asked her, "What has happened Nadia?" Nadia just did not know how to tell a young new mother that her first child was at the death's door and so she did not say anything which did nothing to make Amna feel better. As soon as she had opened the lock on Amna's door she rushed back outside, Amna saw her run towards the open main door and so she followed. Amna walked out the door just to see the lifeless body of her only ray of hope, lying in a puddle of his own blood. She was traumatized; she fell to her knees as tears rolled down her rose red cheeks. She stared at his forever shut eyes as she had a vision of her playing with Hamza, feeding him, laughing with him, dressing him, making his hair, kissing his forehead, pampering him; came to her. She just stared at the lifeless body of her once only reason to live as tears continuously rolled down her cheeks and dripped down her chin onto the wet grassy soil. She put her shaking hands over Hamza's face and slowly run her hands through his bloody hair. She felt his cracked open head as she took her hands out of his silky brown hair. She remembered how she got her son taken away from her and how she did not even have an opportunity to say goodbye. She could not even see him alive for the last time before he was killed. This was the worst imaginable situation for a mother, especially a mother as young as Amna; a twenty four year mother who thought she was going to live her best life once she was married. She still had an image his bid watery, starry eyes in her mind; the eyes that lighten up the darkest of her nights. She put her hands in front of her face and looked at them from both sides before completely blacking out.

Even the most stone hearted person would have felt pity for Amna at this point after all that had happened to her. Samina still did not feel guilty for what she had done, instead, she felt happy to see Amna in pain. Her mother looked at Amna and had confused emotions; she thought she was not going to be able to even handle the sight of her grandson dying but no that it had happened in reality, she was actually okay with it and did not feel an intense fit of distress. Amna was lying unconscious next to her dead six year old child in the tall hay like grass as all her in-laws stood around the mother and the son.

Nadia was sobbing to see such a sight; she cried, "For the love of God take the poor girl inside!" Her loud cry brought everyone's attention towards her and Amna. Nadia struggled to speak as she cried and begged her brother, Ahtasham to take Amna inside the house and call an ambulance. Ahtasham looked at his mother before approaching Amna hesitantly. His mother shouted and forbid him from going near her because the people that were not even present there were not even present there were going to say 'things'. She said that unless any woman was not going to help, Amna had to stay there. Nadia had no choice left, despite being young and not so strong, she had to pick Amna up and take her inside. She knew that her sister Shazia was not going to help and so with tears in her eyes, she wrapped her arms around Amna's unconscious body and lifted her up. She picked Amna's unmade hair off her face and put it back. She then walked in the house and put Amna on the couch as Amna's blood covered hair and hands stained the heather brown couch. Outside, as Nadia took Amna inside, Amna's mother-in-law asked her daughter, Samina what happened. Samina hesitated and then told her mother that she was just picking the cloths off the line and suddenly heard Hamza scream and so she rushed to the edge of the roof and saw him lying dead on the ground. Her mother did not trust her daughter because of the way she had hesitantly told the whole made up story but she did not question her further because she felt like she did not care.

Nadia came out of the house after she laid Amna on the couch and asked her mother to call Khalid and tell him that his son died. What her mother said afterwards shocked Nadia to the core; she said, "Don't you dare try to call Khalid, don't try to tense him while he is earning for us! He will come at the end of this week, he will know himself." She acted like this was not even a big news, she acted like not Amna's first child had died but a fly had been killed; she did not show a bit of distress or care.

Amna woke up in her, in her bed. She looked around and thanked God that her worst nightmare was finally over. She got off her bed and started to walk towards the door to go out of the room. She could not thank God enough that it was just a nightmare or was it? She opened the door and walked out. She noticed some women from the street walking towards her. She thought it was weird that there were guests because no one came to their house much often. They held Amna gently and started to walk her into the other room. Amna got tensed and she did not know what was happening. Then she got intensely tensed when she saw some people sitting in the other room. It was around this time when Amna was so concerned that she started to try and get free of the women's hold.

She started to cry as she further walked inside to the room. She started to wail in distress and never ending pain to see the lifeless, cold and stiff body of her six year old child. She cried in pain, she wailed and screamed in distress. To others all they saw was a woman wildly crying next to her dead son but to Amna as she could see was the times she fed, dressed, and loved him child and then the same child's lifeless stiff body and his forever shut eyes. She shook her self to free herself from the women's hold as she darted towards the corpse of her final hope's corpse. She fell to her knees next to her son's coffin.

Her dirty, rough, wild unmade hair and the scars on her face were a clear sign of what she had been going through for the last couple of months. She sat on her knees and with shaking hands, picked her now late final ray of sunshine in her arms and put him close to herself. She rested his lifeless head on her chest and kissed his head. She kept on kissing and hugging her dead son as much as she could. All she wanted was to go back in time and change it; alas it was not possible. She started to talk to her dead child as if he was still alive and could hear everything. She said, "Don't worry Hamza, we will take you t the hospital and you will get as good as you'll ever be. Nothing has happened, it's all fine. Tell them that your just sleeping, wake up Hamza; they all think you are dead, show mama you're not. Who would do your homework if you keep sleeping like this all day, wake up; remember we had to play as well." Her condition was deplorable.

Her mother-in-law looked at her in disgust and ordered Samina to shut her up because she cared more about what people would say about a mother crying on the death of her first child. She thought that she was being wild and screaming FOR NO REASON. Samina went up to her and held her by her upper arms and tried to console her. She said to Amna, "Look the people are watching, stop it right now! What would they say!?" Ahtasham, dressed in white, walked in the room with his head down and called Samina to a corner and told her that it was time to take the dead body away and bury it. Samina asked Nadia for some help to literally pull Amna away from the coffin.

Amna was sobbing, with Hamza in her arms, holding him close to herself; wanting to never let go of him but alas, it had to be done. Nadia and Samina went to Amna and slowly sat down next to her. The held her tightly by her arms and started to pull her away as Ahtasham and the other men picked up the coffin. Amna looked at everyone hastily and said, "Where are you taking him!? He is alive, he is sleeping! LEAVE HIM! Nadia stop them why aren't they listening to me! STOP THEM" as she clutched on to her son's coffin and they carried him away. Nadia had tears in her eyes, she consoled Amna and kissed her forehead and said, "He is not alive Amna, he is no more." Amna argued with everyone that her son was still alive; maybe she just wanted to convince herself of that. She wailed once again to see her son getting carried away, she saw all her light being killed by the shadows, she saw her final hope to live disappear; she saw her child get carried away. She had to say good bye to the forehead she once kissed, the hands she once held in hers, the eyes that once gleamed to give her hope, the feet she had hoped were going to be so strong one day that not only would pick Hamza himself up but also support her, the cherry lips that once smiled to the rosy cheeks, the mouth that once spoke what was music to Amna's ears; it was timeto say good bye...

CHAPTER EIGHT

Hamza was buried. Half a week had passed now. Khalid arrived home just to be told by his mother that his first and only son was no longer in alive. Amna was still in her room, lying on the floor, curled up in a corner, depressed. Amna had gotten so weak that it was concerning; but only for Nadia because she cared of Amna. Amna could not stop crying; every sight, every scent and every word-everything reminded her of her late son. It was hard for her to even breathe.

"What!" Amna recognized Khalid's voice from outside the room and started to pay attention to what he was saying. She knew he was back; meeting him just did not matter for her anymore. In fact, nothing mattered for her anymore, she just wanted a normal life and now she wanted to end it. Khalid's voice was followed by a mutter of her mother-in-law, "Shhh! God sent him to us and now he called him back, it is the circle of life; IT'S NOT A BIG DEAL." Amna slowly got up, with her messy, dirty unwashed hair, swollen red eyes and tears all over her face, and began to walk out the door. She had heard what her mother-in-law had said. She twisted the door knob slowly and walked out with her head down, whispering, "It's not a big deal." Her messy unwashed hair covered her face before she looked up into her mother-in-law's eyes with her blood red swollen eyes and said in a loud, dominant and furious voice, "It's not a big deal? She says it's not a big deal! My son had died taking all my hopes with him and she says it's not a big deal. My tears have dried up and you say it's not a big deal. It's easy for you to say that woman! You will understand when the same would happen to you. I will never forgive you or your son for what you have done to me, maybe I won't be able to take my revenge but God will!" before her face was slapped with all his force by Khalid making Amna to fall down. He exclaimed, "How dare you talk to my mother like that! I will rip out your tongue; say sorry to my mother, respect her or I know very well how to make you respect her."

Amna was used to this but the agony she was overflowing with because of her child's death made the situation unbearable for her and so, she collapsed and blacked out on the dusty floor. Khalid looked at her with his mother and walked away; leaving Amna on the floor to die. Amna was having a vision while she had blacked out, she saw herself before marriage. She saw all her sisters and her father gathered up in a room in her father's house, having a great laugh. She saw herself, being happy and excited about getting married to the man of her dreams. She saw the day of her marriage as it went before all her loved ones started to abandon her, one by one and all that came out of her mouth was one word, "STAY!" Even when she was unconscious, she was tensed. Nadia had gone to school and it was almost time for her to come back home. Amna was still lying in the middle of the living room, unconscious. An hour passed and no one came to pick Amna off the cold hard stone floor. Nadia came home from school. She used to come with Ahtasham as they both went to the same school and studied in the same grade. Nadia opened the door and walked in to see her sister-in-law lying unconscious on the living room floor. Nadia instantly got concerned about Amna and rushed her way to pick her off the ground. She threw her bag on the couch and sat down on her knees. She took Amna in her arms and put her on the couch next to her school bag. She then turned around to get some water for her and saw her mother standing right behind her. She asked her mother, "Why was Amna on the floor?" Her mother did not reply; she just frowned at her with hatred and disgust and walked away stomping the floor angrily. Nadia was confused and assumed her mother got angry because she had picked Amna off the ground. She was forced to think she did the wrong deed but in reality, she had shown some humanity and helped a poor helpless soul.

Nadia bought Amna a glass of water and started to splash a little amount of water on her face with a flick of her hands. Amna gained consciousness in a while. As soon as she was conscious, she saw Nadia, her only friend, sitting in front of her, caring for her. Amna sat herself up and hugged Nadia as tight as she could and started sniveling. Nadia pat Amna's head to console her and just said, "IT GETS BETTER" to every whimper Amna made. Amna sat back and said, "Why do they hate me so much? What did I ever do to them? Why is this happening to me!?" Nadia just replied with the same line over and over again; she said, "It will all get better."

That night, Amna had a brilliant idea. She decided she was going to tell her father everything and go back to him after leaving Khalid. The only problem was...how was she going to contact her father? She decided to sneak out of her room early in the morning and use the telephone in the living room to make the call to her father; she knew he used to wake up really early before dusk for religious reasons and because he had to go to work. It was an easy to follow plan and nothing could have gone wrong. It was a brilliant and well plotted plan, or was it just what Amna thought of it as? That night, Amna for the first time after her marriage slept with satisfaction because she knew that all her pain was going to end and that she was finally going to go back to her father. She laid her head on her stiff dirty pillow, pulled up her blanked, laid on her right side facing the window, smiled and went to sleep.

The next morning, as she had decided, she woke up before dusk; when it was still dark and the sun was about to start to rise. No one else in the house woke up this early, even not her mother-in-law; they all slept past sunrise. She quietly snuck out of her room and went to the living room where Nadia slept on the floor on a mattress. She tip toed to the small wooden round table over which the telephone sat and started to dial her father's telephone number. She put the receiver next to her ear and waited for her father to pick up.

Her plan was going successful till now. It was not long before her father picked up the phone. Amna started to sob quietly just to think of all what had been done to her by her in-laws, just to think of how her father used to completely adore and pamper her. Her father said, "Who is it?" Amna heard her father's angelic voice and just could not hold her tears in anymore. She burst into tears and sobbing she said, "Father! They don't treat me well. They have destroyed your little flower! Hamza died and I could not even say good bye to him when he was alive because I was locked in my room. I tried standing up to them but Khalid slapped my face so hard that I blacked out and then he just left me there to die! Call me back, I don't want to stay here any longer" She spoke so quickly that her father didn't even get to say a word. He was not ready to hear all this. He could not digest this truth of her most adored and precious flower being treated in the worst and most unimaginable way possible. Tears rolled down his brown wrinkled face as he dropped the receiver of the telephone.

He stepped back from the telephone. His left arm started to ach unbearably, the pain travelled from his arm to his heart and it became impossible for him to stand. He was having a stroke. He threw himself on the bed next to him. He clutched his chest skin between his fingers and palm in pain, hoping it would lessen the pain but it did not. He suffered on the bed until passing out on the same bed.

No one was present in the house; only Haya was and she was in her room; sleeping. Tahir was out all night, working his night job and he was about to come home as soon as the sun rose. Haya used to wake up before Tahir came home but today, because her father was not there to wake her up, she kept on sleeping before hearing a knock on the main metal gate of the house. She got up to the noise of someone knocking the door strongly. She knew it was Tahir and so she darted towards the main gate to open it. She thought it was weird that her father had not waked her up as usual so she decided to go to his room and wake him up. She thought he was so tired of working that he could not get up. She smiled and told Tahir that she was going to her father's room. Tahir joined by saying that he had to discuss something with father. They both went up to the room door and Haya knocked on it.

They both waited for their father to respond until a minute or two passed. Haya asked Tahir if they should go in the room and Tahir agreed. Haya opened the door slowly and walked in. Tahir was behind her. As soon as she entered the room, she screamed and ran to her father who was lying unconscious, curled up with the bed sheets on his bed. Tahir quickly ran in the room to hear Haya's scream. He darted in to see his father on the bed, unconscious, with Haya crying on his side. He tried not to panic and like a sensible person, aimed towards the telephone to call the ambulance. He saw that the telephone receiver was on the floor and the wire was wrapped around his father's leg. This made him curious and he thought, "Who ever made the last call to father is responsible for this" as her picked up the receiver and called the ambulance. He asked Haya to stop crying and told her that everything was going to be fine. Haya could not stop crying. Tahir picked his father up in his arms and took him outside where the ambulance had just arrived. He told Haya to stay at home and check from whom their father received his last call. Haya agreed as Tahir sat in the ambulance with his father and the ambulance drove to the hospital. Haya checked who had made the last call and to her surprise, it was Amna. Haya was still crying. She called Amna but no one picked up.

On the other side, Amna was crying silently. No one was awake yet but it was almost time for them to wake up. The sun had almost arisen. Amna did not know what had happened to her father yet she was afraid she had hurt her father's feelings. Amna walked back into her room and sat on her bed. She cried her eyes out. There were so many unanswered questions in her mind but she just did not know who to ask those questions from; only fate and time could have answered Amna's questions. She let herself fall on the stiff bed she sat on and continued to snivel. She had no idea what had happened to her father because of her call, but it went so perfectly in her mind; how could have anything gone wrong?

In the hospital, Tahir's father was immediately taken to the ICU, leaving Tahir outside to wait. He waited for half an hour before a man came out of the room. He quickly walked up to the man and said, "What happened to my father?" The man turned out to be a doctor, he replied, "Your father has had a stroke, he suffered a severe heart attack but unfortunately, he could not survive it. I am sorry to say, your father has expired; he is no more" as he walked away. Tahir loved his father deeply and thought of him as his greatest and closest friend; in fact, he was the only one Tahir talked to when he needed help, he was his only friend. This made Tahir lose his mind, his brain felt numb as he threw his body on a metal chair at his back. Despite being a strong, masculine man who thought crying was for the feeble, he could not fight the pain and could not hold himself back from shedding a tear. He could not move; time seemed to have stopped for him. He remembered just how last night before he had left the house to go to work; his father had sat down with him and discussed all his issues and problem just like a friend.

He wiped away his tears and got up from the chair. He was not ready to see the dead face of his only friend in the world yet he wanted to see him. He went to the ICU door, knocked on it and entered the room to see a few people standing around his father's bed. A nurse walked up to him and said, "Why are you in here? Your father is still being examined!" "Being examined? What do you mean, a man outside just said that my father had expired?"

The nurse was about to reply when a doctor asked from the background, "What's the matter?" as he walked to Tahir himself. Tahir said, "A man outside said that my father had died but now she is saying that he is still being examined. Please tell me what is going on!" The doctor looked at the nurse and peeped out the glass of the ICU door in search of someone before saying, "Who told you that your father has expired? He has only had a heart attack but is out of danger now. It will take some time for him to get back on his feet but he is out of danger now." Tahir took a sigh of relief as he threw his head back and said, "Thank you God for saving my father." He then said, "How much time would he take to get better so we could take him back home? The doctor said, "It depends. Sometimes it can take as long as two days but if your father is healthy, it might be able to go back home by night falls." Tahir walked out of the room as the doctor returned next to his patient's bed and the nurse closed the door. Khalid came back to his seat and sat down. He once again thanked God for his father was still alive. He was happy but Haya had no idea what had happened; she was still at home, crying. She tried to call Tahir but his phone was set on silent and so he did not receive the call. This tensed Haya even more.

This was in no matter in comparison to what Amna was suffering from. She was dying from inside, she was empty; all that she had had been forced away from her. She was depressed but no one understood that. But still she had some hope; she knew everything was going to get better soon because she thought her father was going to call her back to his home. She was satisfied but at the same time she was worried about why had her father dropped the phone and not answered. She felt bad for breaking her father's heart but it was something she had to do to end her pain; not that she was selfish, she just wanted for all her pain to end already and she knew with the end of her pain; her father's pain would end as well. The day passed, luckily, Tahir had just received his pay and so it was not a problem for him to pay the hospital. He lovingly took his father home by the end of the night and finally, Haya got to know all what had happened to her father but she was just thankful that her father was well and alive. The doctor had suggested their father nothing but a healthy diet and some exercise to keep his heart healthy.

Amna on the other hand, was finally satisfied that her troubles were going to come to a halt. She slept once again with satisfaction. The next day, Tahir went to work and told Haya that she had to skip school for a day or two and stay at home with father to care for him; Haya agreed. Haya loved her father a lot and her father loved her even more. Her father remembered each and everything Amna had said and so he was still worried about what to do; he could not just leave Amna with her in-laws to suffer. He decided that he was going to call her back. She was his most beautiful and favorite daughter and he just could not bear all that her in-laws were doing to her. Haya also was curious to know what was that Amna said to her father that caused him to get so upset that he suffered a heart attack.

Her father was lying on his small bed in his small beige colored room. She walked up to his bed and sat on her knees besides his bed. He turned his head to look at her. She said, "Father, I wanted to ask you something. Can I?"He replied, "Well of course you can my princess." She asked, "Father, why had Amna called you the other day? That was the last call you received before you had a stroke and the receiver was not even put back on the phone so I assume perhaps something she said was the reason for your heart attack. Is it so?" Her father hesitated for a while but then decided to tell her everything honestly. He told her, "Haya, Amna is not happy with her in-laws; Khalid hit her face, Hamza died and they treat her like a slave-rather even worse. I have decided I am going to call her back and get her divorced from Khalid. She is still young; she will find a new and better person to spend her life with." Haya repeated only one thing with emphasis; she said, "HAMZA DIED! HOW?" her father told her that Amna had not told him how her son died, she just told him that he died. Haya agreed with her father and told him that it was going to be best if he called Amna back to him.

He asked Haya to bring the phone to her. Haya did so and he dialed Khalid's telephone number. Amna's mother-in-law picked up and asked who it was calling. Amna's father was mad; he felt hatred for his daughter in her mother-in-law's voice. He did not answer her question, he in a fit of fury, told her that he knew everything that they were doing to his daughter and that he was going to get his daughter divorced and call her back to him. Amna's mother-in-law got literally frightened; Amna's father was a lion, especially when it came to protecting his daughters. He was not someone who would act masculine to be dominant over women, he was furious. Her mother-in-law could not speak a word; she stood there holding the receiver in her trembling hands silently. He said, "She is not alone! I stand with her as her greatest support and don't you forget that!" He slammed down the receiver of the telephone and ended the call. Amna's mother-in-law was absolutely terrified, she was a person who could only oppress the weak but could not face the strong and that was exactly what Amna's father was; strong.

Amna was sitting in her room. Her mother-in-law knocked the door for the very first time and asked for her permission to come in. Amna was confused and she still thought that her mother-in-law was maybe taunting her but she did not sense irony in her tone of speaking. She felt like her mother-in-law was scared which was very weird to Amna. Amna quickly got up and opened the door. Her mother-in-law had turned pale; she said, "Amna child, why did you open the door? I could have done it myself sweetie." Amna was shocked; she could not digest all this. She felt awkward and thought she was dreaming. Amna asked her what had happened. Her mother-in-law asked her to sit down on the bed. After they had sat down, her mother-in-law said, "Amna, did you call your father? He was saying that we don't treat you right. Honey you should have told me if you needed something; why did you call your father?"

Amna felt brave, she knew her father had called her mother-in-law and that was the reason she was scared. She said, "NEEDED SOMETHING! You have treated me in the way no one would even treat a dog. You have beaten me; you have left me hungry for days! What else could you have done and yet you say I could have just told you if I needed something? You disgust me woman!" Normally, her mother-in-law would have hit her if she would have said so much in front of her but now, things had changed. Amna was fearless now. Her mother-in-law was enraged by the way Amna spoke but she feared to do anything, she just left the room without saying anything.

The next day, Amna's father had made up his mind to go get his daughter back from those stone hearted people. He told this to Haya but Haya strictly went against his plan; she thought her father's health condition did not support travelling. She said that they were going to go but in a week and not before that but her father was not ready to leave Amna a minute more with those people but when Haya insisted, he agreed with his heaviest heart. Tahir did not know of his father's plan or about what was happening to Amna. Tahir's father had to earn but it was not possible for him to do so in that condition; of course he 'knew' he was fine but his children actually knew what his condition was yet he did not hold back from sneaking out for work. It had only been a day or two and he had already left for work.

That day, he had another, much worse stroke because instead of getting rest he wanted to get money to help Amna settle. Lifting weight turned out to cause a much worse impact on his body. He suffered another heart attack. One of his co-workers took him to the hospital and called Tahir and told him what had happened. Haya could not stop him from leaving the house because he left earlier than when Haya woke up. As much as Tahir was mad at Haya for being careless, he was even more worried about his father.

This time the doctors told Tahir that the stroke was much worse and that it could be fatal. The doctor further told Tahir that his father was going to stay in what they called, 'the danger zone' for a couple of hours. Time stopped for Tahir, it seemed to stand still because he was so tensed and worried about so many things but the top most being his father. Only one thing that the doctor said was on his mind, "IT COULD BE FATAL" Khalid was crying; he tried not to but he could not help himself. He just prayed to God that he would save his father's life again.

Haya was confused and scared about where her father had gone. She knew that Tahir would not spare her for being so careless but she certainly did not know what had happened in reality. She called Khalid and Khalid in a fit of fury yelled at her on the phone as he sobbed. Haya's heart beat dropped to hear that her father had another heart attack. She remembered that one of her teachors had passed away after she had had a second stroke. Her head ached to have this thought as her eyes started fill up with tears. She thought she was no longer going stay at home; she wanted to go to the hospital to see her father for herself but alas she was not 'allowed' by her brother to do so.

In the hospital, Tahir waited to hear anything from the doctor before a nurse walked out his father's. Tahir ran up to her and asked her about his father. The nurse told him that his father's condition was critical; it was difficult for him to survive. He did not believe what he was told because he remembered what had happened last time. He did not hesitate to enter the ICU room where his father was. He walked up to the doctor next to his father and asked him the same thing. He thought the doctor was going to tell him that the nurse lied and she knew nothing because his father was perfectly fine and they were going to discharge him by the night.

The doctor said, "I am sorry to say this, but your father expired the moment he had a stroke; the stroke was very intense. We tried our best in saving his life but we couldn't. Tahir did not want to believe this, he asked another doctor just to hear the sad bitter reality once more. He felt a sudden feeling of emptiness, his heart beat dropped as all the doctors left him alone in the room with the dead body of his father. He walked to the left side of his father's bed and sat down on his knees. Tears rolled down his eyes as he took his father's old brown wrinkled hand in his. He looked at his father's forever shut eyes with a feeling of loneliness. He stared to talk to his dead friend; knowing he was not able to hear anything he said. He addressed his father and said, "Father, why did you leave me alone in this cruel, dark world? You were my only companion, my only friend; I thought you were never going to leave me alone like the others but you abandoned me just like them? Why? Haya was so young; how will she feel when she hears that you left us just like the rest of the selfish world? You were our only well wisher, our strongest back bone; why did you have to go like this without any warning? Why did you have to go somewhere where we can't come to meet you, where we can't see you? Why father? Tell me why!?" He threw his head down in despair and he sobbed until he could not do so anymore.

At home, Haya was unaware of her father's death. She was still praying for her father's life; hoping he would come back home alive. Little she knew; her father had already crossed the rainbow bridge. Her father was the only protection she had; even her brother did not understand her problem, only her father did.

Tahir decided to call Haya and tell her everything. Haya was sitting next to the telephone; waiting for Tahir to call and tell her that he was bringing father home. Tahir called and when Haya picked up the phone, he said, "Haya, I have bad news…" Haya's heart beat dropped. Without hearing another single word, she started to sob. She felt despair and distress in Tahir's voice. She already knew what the 'bad news' was. Tahir heard Haya's cry and started to cry himself. He sobbed as he told Haya that their father was no more. Haya let out a loud wail of pain and distress to hear this. Tahir understood his pain. He told her that he was bringing their father's dead body home for the funeral. Even saying those words made him cry but alas, he had to do it; after all, he was the elder son and now had to run the house. Haya put down the receiver and fell to her knees. She wailed loudly as she complained, "Why God? Why did you do this to me? Did you not hear all my prayers? Did they all end in smoke?" She pulled her hair as she cried.

Their neighbors heard her cries and so they came to ask her what had happened. Haya could not utter a single word. She tried to tell them that her father had passed away but no one could make out a single word she spoke. The woman from her neighbors sat Haya down on the bed and calmed her down. Haya was still sobbing but at least she was not wailing anymore. The woman asked her again, "Haya, what happened and where is your father?" Haya could not control herself; she burst into tears and yelled, "HE IS GONE! He is not coming back. He is gone" and started to wail again. The woman next to her pat her shoulder to consol her and put Haya's head on her shoulder and continued to pat her head to consol her. Haya wailed and cried until she passed out on the woman's shoulder.

An hour passed, Tahir bought his father home in

an ambulance. Haya had passed out and had still not gained consciousness. Tahir laid his father's dead body on his bed and went to get a coffin for the burial of his father's lifeless body. In an hour or so, before her brother had come home, Haya got back conscious. The women from the neighborhood told her not to go see her father but she did not listen; though she knew she was not going to be able to handle to see her father's dead face, his shut eyes and his lips that could no longer speak to support and love her. She walked to him and hugged his dead body as she cried and wailed. All the women thought that it was 'unethical and rude' for her to do so. They thought it was bad and 'rude' for an almost fifteen year old daughter to cry over her dead father's body; the father who was the only one who understood and loved her deeply. The women decided it would be best to take her away and call Tahir to come quickly. All of the women grasped Haya by her arms and took her away to another room. She reached out to grasp her father's cloths or his hand but she failed. She was forced to get away from her father and could not even say her longest final good bye.

The funeral passed, they buried their father. Everyone left the grave except Tahir; he stayed there, regardless of everyone's judgment. He cried. This was his breaking point; he could not bear more pain. He threw his head down and just wept; he did not know what to say or what to do, his brain felt numb. Haya on the other hand, could not even see her father for the very first time because apparently it was not what 'cultured' girls do.

Tahir came back home and consoled Haya; he

made it very clear to her as well that he was the in charge of the house now and she had to agree to whatever he said no matter how she felt about it. Haya was still in deep trauma; she did not know how to respond to anything that Tahir said or asked her and Tahir understood that very well because he suffered the same pain as his sister. All he wanted to ask her was, "Why had their father left for work? Who had called the father the day he had his first stroke and what had the caller said that caused the stroke?" Tahir left her in her room like she was because he knew that nothing he said or did was going to make Haya feel better. He skipped work for a few days. The next day, he came to Haya; who was curled up in a corner of her father's room as she clutched her father's shirt in her hands. Tahir felt her pain and so he did not want to say something intense in front of her that would possibly make her condition worse but he needed answers. He walked to her slowly, sat down and picked her up and sat her down on the ground in front of him. He said, "Haya, I know we are going through some harsh times right now and I can feel your pain but we need to find the person who has done this to father! I know you checked the telephone for the caller who called father before his stroke, just tell me his or her name and I will do the rest. Also, did father discuss with you what had he gone to work? Because I know he did not do so to run the house, he did so for reasons unknown to me but maybe you know why; you will have to tell me honestly if you want the person who did this to father to suffer just like our father did."

Haya knew the most precise answers to all those

questions but it took her a long time to decide what to say. She did not know what to say and what to hide but she knew that truth always solves every problem in the long run; at least more than white lies could ever do. She knew what to do. She told Tahir everything honestly; from Amna's deplorable condition because of her in-laws to her assumption about why her father had gone to work. She even told him that her father was going to call Amna back and get her divorced by Khalid because he just could not bear his precious flower being stepped on like the way her in-laws were torturing her. Tahir was enraged to hear this. He considered Amna to be the murderer of her own father. He knew exactly what to do.

CHAPTER NINE

Amna was now confident, brave and fearless because she believed her father was there to support her and he was soon going to call her back. Not one of her in-laws dared to say a word to her face; of course they said a lot behind her back but they did not have a bit of courage that would allow them to say anything to her face because they knew that her father now knew each and everything and was going to tear them apart if there came another harm to her daughter just like the lion he was. Amna was finally getting the respect she was promised and that she deserved.

It had just been a day since Amna had started enjoying her life a little because of the way she was being treated with respect and care before a letter came. She knew the letter was going to be addressed to her and was going to be from her home. She thought the letter was going to be written by her father in which he was going to call her back to him. She was happier than ever that now she was finally going back to her father, all her pain was about to end; everything was going to get better now. She unsealed the envelope in which came the letter. By her first look, she thought the writing did not belong to her father but then again she thought it was just because she had not read her father's writing for a really long time. She finally started reading the letter; she read,

Amna,

I know that you called father the other day to tell himabout what is happening to you in that house. Its like you only want your pain to end; father had a stroke after your call. We had to take him to the hospital. He wanted to call you back to him because of all that you said your in-laws did to you. He went to work to earn money for you and had another stroke which killed him. Consider yourself the murderer of your own father Amna. Women of our family when are once married, don't come back to their parent's home.Consider the doors of this house shut for you forever so it is better if you learn to live with your in-laws. That is your only home now.

-Tahir

Amna's heart beat dropped to hear this. She burst into tears to read about her father; the father who was her last hope, her only support; he was gone now and her brother blamed it on her. She was certainly not ready for this. She dropped the piece of paper from her hands as tears rolled down her cheeks and fell down along with the letter she had just read. There was som much written in that letter that

Amna's mind just could not dijest all that had been scribbled by her very own brother on the piece of paper. She looked around her to see if anyone saw her cry because she knew that if her in-laws got to know that her father had passed away, they were going to start treating her the same way as they used to; rather they were going to treat her even worse now that they know that Amna had nowhere to go and that she was helpless. Amna quickly wiped away her tears with her sleeves and saved all her tears to weep in her room, alone. Shw picked up the letter and hid every trace of it so that no one was going to be able to know that a letter had even arrived and then she went to her room. She threw herself on her bed and cried. She held her mouth shut so that she could not let out a wail. She cried in pain and felt forlorn.

It was not long before her mother-in-law noticed that Amna had been in her room for quiet a while. She went up to Amna's bedroom door and stood quietely close to it. She put her ear next to the door and listened carefully. At first, she heard nothing but then as she listened more carefully and closely, she heard feable, quietened cries. She got shocked and stepped back from the door in surprise. She thought it was just her mind playing tricks on her so she put her ear next to the door again and listened again; she heard even more cries. She got scared because she thought that Amna was crying because she or her daughter had again did something wrong or painful to Amna. She was scared her father was going to take them to court for hitting such a young girl so bad that she got scars and bruises. She knocked the door and asked for Amna's permission to come in. Amna could not answer so her mother-in-law just came in without asking again. She saw that Amna was curled up on her bed. As soon as Amna noticed that her mother-in-law had walked in the room, she quickly sat up and wiped away her tears.

Her mother-in-law came closer to her, sat down next to her and asked her if she had done anything wrong. Amna shook her head and said no. Her mother-in-law noticed that there was a piece of paper in Amna's hands. She asked Amna about it, "What's that piece of paper in your hand, Amna?" Amna clutched the paper in her hands tighter and said it was nothing. Her mother-in-law understood that Amna was hiding something from her. Her mother-in-law asked again, "Amna, what is that you're holding in your hand? Show it to me." Amna did not want to do so but she had no choice. The truth was going to reveal itself one way or another so Amna thought it would be best if she revealed it earlier. She knew that even if she hid the reality from her in-law, they were eventually going to come to know of it and when they did, they were going to behave even worse with Amna so Amna had no other better option. With shaking hands, Amna handed over the piece of paper in her hands to her mother-in-law. Her mother-in-law opened the piece of paper and squinted at it to read what was written on it. Amna cried as a wide smile of joy invaded her mother-in-law's face.

After she was done reading, she looked at Amna with pride, joy and a smile on her wrinkled face to claim her victory. Amna looked down to her crossed legs to show her mother-in-law that she had failed and lost all hope. But that was not all, her mother-in-law and her sister-in-law were going to take revenge on Amna for making them be nice to her for all those days, for acting like she was the ruler of everything; which she felt like once she knew her father stood with her but alas he was gone now and not even the strongest of earthly powers could bring him back.

Her mother-in-law got up, crumbled up the letter into a ball and threw it at Amna's face and then walked out the room laughing. Now that her mother-in-law had found out, Amna had nothing to hide; she let out a long, painful wail as she threw herself back and accidently hit her boney back on the old wooden carved bed back. Her mother-in-law walked back in and said, "Keep your 'pain and grief' to yourself; let us enjoy this great moment of victory and finally freedom." She then again walked out the room after letting out a huge loud laughter. Amna put her both hands on her moth and shut it closed as she cried. Her eyes turned red as an ocean of tears rolled out her eyes and down her once rose red cheeks.

Her mother-in-law was beyond happy to hear of Amna's father's death whereas Amna wished for her own death; she wanted it all to end already even if the cost for it was her own life. How many more struggles, pains and troubles had fate planed for her until she could finally live in peace. Perhaps she was not going to get any peace; at least not in this life. Her mother-in-law darted towards the telephone and called her daughter Shazia to tell her of this 'good news'. This news had a little but a happy effect on Shazia. She really did not care because she met Amna so little but still flames of hatred burnt for Amna in her heart and so she was quite happy. Then her mother-in-law called

Khalid to tell him of this. She dialed his phone number and to her complete surprise, a woman picked up the phone and asked about the identity of the called. Her mother-in-law said, "Sorry, I must have dialed the wrong number" as she put down the receiver of the telephone.

She dialed the number again; more carefully this time and put the receiver next to her ear waiting for Khalid to pick up. This time, again she heard the same female's voice on the other side of the line. This took her by surprise; she was sure that this time she had dialed the correct number which belonged to her son Khalid. She was confused why a woman was picking up her son's phone again and again so she asked, "Who are you? Where is my son Khalid?" The woman on the other side of the line suddenly changed her tone from harsh to a sweeter tone. She said, "Mot..." but before she could complete saying even a single word, Khalid came running and snatched the phone from her. He quickly put his phone next to his ear and said, "Hello? Who is it?" His mother did not reply to his question but rather she posed a counter question as she asked, "Khalid! Who was that woman that picked up the phone!?"

Khalid murmured confusedly and hesitantly as he said, "Uh... mother...uh she was...uh...the maid at my house." His mother was still not satisfied by her son's answer. She was doubtful as there was an awkward silence between them on the phone. Khalid seemed scared and like he wanted to keep something hidden from his mother which was unknown to everyone except him. His mother was quite excited to tell him about the great news of Amna's father's death that she did not pay much attention to what had just happened. She continued, "I have good news for you my son! We are finally free to do whatever we want without the fear of anyone. He is dead; Amna's father is dead. He is gone." Khalid could not believe his ears for what he heard was great unbelievable news. He was beyond happy and exited. All the possible ways they could hurt Amna to get revenge on her circled their minds.

Amna on the other hand was in her room, trying to get over what had just happened; she had to do so for she knew what was coming for her from the side of her in-laws and her husband for her but the pain was too big to come over in such a short period of time. Amna's in-laws started to behave the way they used to; rather even worse. They used to hit her with metal rods and burn her skin with red hot metal rods when she used to be unable to do something for them or even got late in doing the chores. Amna became a slave rather than wife. Even the worst land lords would not have treated their slaves in the way Amna was treated. She was a living dead body who had died completely from her inside. She had no will to live or to do anything; she was just a dead slave who could just do work for people.

It was not long before she got used to getting burnt or hit by metal rods; it did hurt her anymore rather nothing did. The only way she cried was silent and alone; hidden from everyone. She hated expressing her pain to people who she knew were not going to care for it. Amna thought of suicide several times but then again something stopped herself from ending her life. Perhaps fate made her do it; for it had

something special in mind for the young unfortunate
soul.

CHAPTER TEN

A year passed. Amna's life did not get any better; instead it got worse as each miserable day passed. Amna had nothing to do except serving her in-laws. It was not long before Amna was expecting a child. Once again, the house bloomed up with joy. Amna slowly started coming towards life from the depths of death. Her mother-in-law wanted it to be a son; obviously just like every other person did but Amna just wanted a healthy child, regardless of the child's gender because that was what she was taught by her father; never to discriminate genders. Amna was once again treated in a better way because her mother-in-law thought that Amna's new child was going to be her grandson. Amna knew what was going to happen afterwards so she tried not to get used to the services her in-laws provided her with. Of course Nadia helped and cared for her without any reason and Samina did not care about anyone except herself; anything related to Amna was something she was least bothered by at all times. The main people who started to care for Amna intensely was her mother-in-law. Even Khalid did not seem to get excited about having a baby boy. Amna finally had a child. Everyone was excited to see the little baby boy until it was revealed that it was not a baby boy rather a precious baby girl. Their smiles turned to frowns, their excitement and happiness turned to frustration. The mother-in-law fell from cloud nine as flames of anger burst in her mind; the flames that burnt to burn Amna down to ashes. Khalid had not bothered coming home to see his new child and his mother now thought that he was right for not coming home to see the birth of such an inferior creature. Khalid told everyone he was 'busy in work' and that was the reason he could not come home.

Amna loved her daughter and had already thought of her name before her birth despite everyone's prediction of her child being a boy. She named her first daughter 'Noor' which roughly translates to 'light'. Amna knew Noor was going to bring the light of hope and bliss into her life. As every mother, Amna felt Noor as her most prized possession. On the other hand, her mother-in-law was disgusted by Amna and her daughter. She did not want to keep the daughter rather she wanted to send her away. She even thought of selling the feeble newborn to possibly anyone who needed a baby for any reasons which she did not care of.

Nadia and Ahtasham were obviously with their mother in the hospital. Their mother sent Nadia to a corner as she asked Ahtasham to come with her to discuss something. She said in a low voice, "Ahtasham, you see, girls are weak and useless. We will just tell Amna that her child died instantly after death; she has not seen her daughter for herself till now, only the doctor has informed her about it. We will just pay the doctor to keep his mouth shut." Ahtasham looked at his mother in shook. He knew she hated her daughter-in-law but he had never thought she could have been this evil. He saw the devil in his mother's eyes; forcing her to ruin Amna's life forever. He forbid her from doing so. He was actually quite scared of his mother at this moment, he stepped a step or two back from him mother; shaking his head in disappointment and disagreement. His mother looked at him in disgust as she frowned at him for a while as he turned back and walked to Nadia to tell her about what their mother had just said.

A week passed, Amna acted like a wild cat protecting her cub when anyone even said of taking Noor away from her. Khalid had still not seen or even heard of his new daughter; neither did he pick up call nor did he come to visit as another stressful week passed. Amna knew what it felt to have to let go of a child and she was not going to make the same mistake again. She was wiser now; she knew how to act. The storm filled her lungs with water but it also taught her to breathe underwater. Nadia and Ahtasham had promised Amna that they were not going to let anything happen to Noor. They had seen the pain of a mother on the death of her first child; they did not want that to happen again so they decided to stay alert from the beginning.

A month passed and now finally, Khalid was 'not busy' and so he decided to come home to see his new child. He had no idea whether it was a boy or a girl but being a backward, narrow-minded man that he was; he wanted it to be his son. He did not know who or what awaited him in his house as his child. Amna's mother-in-law decided she was not going to neither talk nor reply to anything Nadia, Ahtasham or Amna said. She even stopped cooking them food. She forced them to starve for days but of course Ahtasham and Nadia used to ask for money from their pals and friends and bring food for the little innocent baby.

Khalid arrived home in the middle of a dark windy night. His mother told him about the gender of his child and he was anything but pleased. She further told him how she wanted to get rid of the useless creature but her own children stopped her. A master plan popped up in Khalid's head. Everyone was asleep yet he whispered the plan in his mother's ear. They both smiled with satisfaction. His mother was happy; knowing her son Khalid was finally going to take care of Amna's son. Neither did she accept Noor as her granddaughter nor did Khalid consider her his daughter. Khalid tip toed to Amna's and his bedroom in the dim heather yellow light of the blinking bulb in the living room.

His mother watched him go as she watched him from across the room. He carefully opened the door to the room. Amna was asleep on the bed next to Noor who was sleeping content like an angel she was. The devil smiled through Khalid's lips as he slowly put his arms towards Noor. He turned his head to check if his so called wife was still asleep and yes, to his pleasure, she still was. He had to make sure that Noor did not cry or wake up Amna and he had a plan to take care of that as well. He forwarded his big hairy hand towards Noor's angelic face. He slowly put his hand nearer and nearer to Noor's face until finally he acted upon his plan, he clutched Noor's soft little head in his big hairy hand. He put force on her mouth; making sure not a single cry for help escaped her mouth. He put both of his hands over her mouth to make sure he succeeded in his mission to get rid of that nasty foul creature.

It did not take very long for the little angle to cross the rainbow bridge and go back to the creator from whom she came from. Khalid slowly pulled back his bands to himself and looked at what seemed to be the lifeless face of an almost three weak old feeble child; his very own child. He made sure that she was dead; he put his two fingers in front of her nose to check if she was breathing and to his joy and bliss, she was not. He walked backwards from the cradle as he moved out of the door. He shut the door quietly as he turned back and walked to his mother. He let out a sigh of relief as he said, "It's done; she is gone forever!" His mother smiled at him as he smiled back. He told her that this way, they could just say that she died a natural death and they won't get in trouble. His mother agreed. She kissed him on his forehead as she told him to go sleep on the couch so that Amna would not get doubtful about him killing Noor. He smiled back at her as his mother walked away into her room. The baby girl who was born three weeks ago to be the ray of hope for Amna had been brutally murdered by her own father; Amna's hopes and dreams had been brutally murdered by her own partner.

The dark night passed; hiding the most brutal secrets with its darkness as it carried them along with it. The mourning came as Amna woke up to the dusk. She smiled as she got up and walked to her daughter's cradle. She looked down at her face and leaned over. She kissed her cheek and then her forehead with eternal love and adoration. She then took her small chubby hand into hers and held it. She felt that Noor was cold; she assumed maybe it was because of the weather despite the weather being quite humid. She adjusted Noor in her blanket and then went to the kitchen to milk for the little child. She had hidden some evaporated milk powder in the back of the cupboard so that her mother-in-law would not see it. Her mother-in-law had hidden all food items in order to starve Amna and Noor. Amna prepared the milk for her under the dim light of the rising sun that entered the kitchen through the small window at the top of a wall. She did not turn on any lights so that no one would see her. She was happy; after a long time, she was finally blissful. She was happy that now she had a child and she knew she was going to bring her up in the best way possible. She kept a wide smile of satisfaction on her face as she walked back into her room to feed Noor. She picked up

Noor in her arms and said, "Wake up Noor; it's time for your milk darling." She slowly pat her head to wake her up. Noor used to wake up instantly and did not sleep a lot. This made Amna worried; she started to shake Noor a little to wake her up. Upon no response from her daughter, she panicked. She yelled, "Nadia!" Nadia had just waked up. On hearing Amna's scream, she rushed to her room. She slammed open the door and ran to Amna and asked, "What happened!? Is everything alright?" Amna had started to cry by this time; she said, "Noor is not waking up! She is not waking up Nadia!" Nadia quickly took Noor in her hands and said, "Wake up Noor, look your mother is so tensed" as she gently shook her. Amna's cries got stronger and louder when she saw that Noor was absolutely unresponsive. Amna wailed; to hear her loud painful wail, everyone in the house woke up. Ahtasham came rushing in her room still dressed in his shabby cream white nightwear. He saw Nadia and Amna, both crying next to each other as Nadia held Noor in her hands. Without caring about what his mother would think about him helping Amna, he darted towards her and said, "What happened?" Neither Amna nor Nadia answered; they both couldn't say anything because they were crying. Amna could only say one thing, "She won't wake up!"

Meanwhile, Khalid and his mother were in the living room; listening to everything. They knew what had happened and they were least bothered by it. They had to act like they did not know what happened so that Amna would not take them to court; even if they did not let Amna do it, Ahtasham would have done it because he feared God and believed in Karma. Khalid and his mother discussed in a low voice what they had to do next as Amna and Nadia cried in the background. Ahtasham's first doubt was his mother because he remembered how his mother wanted to get rid of Noor in the first place and his mother not coming to see what had happened added to his suspicion. Khalid got up with his mother as they both slowly walked to Amna's room. Ahtasham looked at them from a distance; with suspicion and doubt in his eyes he stared at them. His mother came in the room first and said, "Shut up! Everyone is listening. What will everyone from the street say? That this house is full of sad depressed women? That I don't treat my daughter-in-law well? Shut up, what is the matter?" She took Noor in her arms and looked at her.

Despite her trying her best to not express her deep eternal hatred for the baby, she still had a visible grin on her face as she looked at the little baby with disgust. Ahtasham's doubt had been getting stronger and stronger as every painful moment passed. Khalid acted as if he was highly concerned; he ran up to the little girl, snatched her from his mother's arms and took her in his arms. He put his fingers in front of her nose and told everyone that she was not breathing as he faked panic. He then put his ear on her chest to act like he was trying to listen to her heart beat. After a while of silence in the room as Khalid pretended to listen to his dead daughter's heart beat, he slowly picked his head back up and said, " She is no more" as he faked a cry. He then stopped faking cries and walked back and stood with his mother. Amna was certainly not ready for the death of her Noor, the death of her light, the death of her sunshine, the death of her only left hope; she was not ready.   As soon as she heard this tragic news, her knees could not hold the weight of her sad, unfortunate body and she fell down on the hard stoned floor as she hit her head on the ground. She had blacked out; she hit her head down on the floor as she cracked her head open. At first, everyone just looked at Amna as Nadia cried but as soon as they saw blood, Nadia screamed. Ahtasham bent down to pick her up off the ground as Khalid and his mother looked at them. As soon as Ahtasham touched Amna's arm to pick her up; Khalid got offended that another man dared to touch his wife; the wife who he treated like trash. He slapped Ahtasham so hard that Ahtasham fell aside. Khalid was around forty while his wife was almost twenty three. He had married an underage girl. In the vision of an educated person, he was considered a pedophile for marrying a girl half his age but in the eyes of his mother and the uneducated mindless society, he was a 'successful' man.

Ahtasham looked at Khalid for a long while as Khalid looked at him furiously with hatred and disgust. Ahtasham broke down; he broke down to see the constant seemingly never ending pain of such a young mother, he broke down to see the cruel face his mother had been hiding behind her smiles, he broke down to see how unconcerned Khalid was to see his wife possibly die, he broke down to see the death of a newborn angel, he broke down to see Khalid's true colors; he broke

down. Khalid exclaimed, "How dare you! How dare you touch my wife! If needed, I myself will pick her up. Who gave you the right to touch her?" He then tried to approach Amna to pick her up but his mother stopped him. Noor was in Nadia's arms. Her mother ordered her to pick Amna up. Nadia picked Amna up as her hands got red by the blood of a tortured mother. Ahtasham quietly shed a tear on the floor next to the bed. His mother looked at him in disgust as she called him a feminine useless piece of trash. Khalid was in her eyes a brave, masculine man; perhaps she thought forcing your power over women meant being masculine. Perhaps she was wrong but there was no one courageous enough to tell her that.

CHAPTER ELEVEN

Amna had lost another child. The murderer's face was hidden behind the curtains of white lies. Amna had lost all will live; she did not care if God restricted suicide, she was ready to end all this. If fate was not going to better her life, she was going to end it herself. It was not that Amna had always been like this, she had always been so full of life but now she had absolutely no reason to continue her life.

Amna did not want to become a mother again for she did not want to kill another baby. Yet fate had planed something very different for her. Despite her will to die and never have another child ever again, she had a child. It seemed like her fate was just playing with her; putting her through the worst conditions and not making the sun of good times rise in her life. Fate was giving her constant dark nights without any sign of a new fresh morning light ever ending the eternal darkness of her life.

She had another daughter. Amna did not want her; she wanted to give her away to someone who would keep her safe and sound. She as herself did not want to keep the daughter but the mother inside of her could not have bared to separate the little child from her for even a split second. She was left with no choice but to keep the child to herself. But that was certainly not what her in-laws wanted. They hated the little baby. They forced Amna to send her daughter away but Amna rebelled against all what they said. She kept her safe and sound from the cruel world. Ahtasham had realized over time who what killed Noor and so he advised Amna to lock her doors before she went to sleep. Amna did not know why he said that but she did it anyways; she did not want any harm to come to her daughter.

A few years passed. Amna's daughter, Ayesha, was now eleven years old. One day, Khalid came home on a week day. This was weird because it was rare when he came home even on weekends. Khalid did not close the door as he stepped in everyone had gathered around him in the living room to meet and greet him. He seemed to be confused and scared. He was literally sweating as he looked around at everyone from the corner of his eyes. He was hiding something and it was obvious. His mother asked him to close the door; as a reply her said, "Mother, I have something to tell you."

Everyone's eyes were on Khalid and their ears were attentive towards what he said. His mother said, "Ok, whatever it is that you want to say we can sit and talk, just close the door." He did not pay much heed to what his mother said. Khalid was almost above forty years of age and had anger issues. Over time, he had gotten mentally upset; he was mentally upset on the time he was married but his mental conditions were not bought into light by his family members and neither was his age. His upset mental condition was the reason he could not make decisions of his own and mostly only did what his mother said. That was also the reason why he used to hit Amna, burn her, cut her. His cranial condition was also the reason he did not think twice while brutally murdering his daughter otherwise not even a murderer could have killed that young of a baby.

He further said, "Mother you may want to sit down, in fact you all should sit down." Everyone sat on the couch; Amna had been told where she belonged so she went and sat on the ground next to the couch in everyone's feet. Khalid looked down and hesitantly and slowly said, "Everyone, meet Fauzia, my wife…" Everyone gasped as his mother angrily stood up and a middle aged woman walked in the house with her head bent down. Amna stared at her for a while. This did not hurt her at all. She just did not seem to care. Her mother exclaimed, "Khalid! What kind of joke is this!? Who is this woman?" The woman told everyone of her identity, "I am Fauzia, Khalid's wife!" as she raised her head and looked straight into her mother-in-law's eyes. Her mother-in-law frowned as she gasped and said, "How is she talking to me Khalid! If she is your wife does she not know who I am how she is going to talk to me?" She was expecting Khalid to possibly slab Fauzia for talking to her in such disrespectful manner. Khalid looked at Fauzia and then looked at his mother and said, "Mother, she has not said anything wrong, it would be good if you learn that your time is over. It's her time to give orders and get respect. You must learn your place now; times have changed." His mother was confused to hear what Khalid had just said to her. He was a whole new person. He had changed and it was unbelievable. Fauzia smiled as she looked at everyone; telling everyone that she was ruler now, she had the power to order now. Khalid had never done this for Amna and that was the only thing that shocked Amna. She just sat in her place on the floor as she stared at her husband's new wife.

Everyone had told Amna that their financial states were not stable but suddenly now Khalid could afford the addition of a new adult in the family and it was completely fine with everyone. No one dared to say anything; not even Khalid's mother. Now she had come to know about the identity of the woman who had picked up Khalid's phone the last time she had called him. No one objected anything; a lion's wife is a lioness, a rooster's wife is always a hen; weak and feeble. Khalid was a rooster when he married Amna but now for some reason he was a dominant lion. Perhaps it was because of Fauzia; maybe she had put him under a spell because the change that came in Khalid seemed impossible to come naturally.

Ayesha had to grow up over night for she was

born during the darkest night's thunderstorms. She did not have anything that one has upon birth; she craved the love that comes with life. Despite her young age of mere eleven, she acted like a mature person. She learnt to do most of the house chores a kid her age could never even think of doing. Amna's heart burnt to see her daughter struggle like this. Amna cried tears of pain to see her daughter miss out on every little thing she was supposed to enjoy at her age. She knew this was not the way Ayesha was supposed to live her life. Her in-laws did not even let her go to school. She wanted to study; she wanted to do everything every other girl her age did. She was used by everyone but most important she and her mother both were bound to serve Fauzia or else Khalid had threatened Amna that he was going to divorce her. From giving her foot massages to cleaning her cloths, everything was the mother and daughter's duty. Amna had to sift to the living room so that Fauzia could stay in her room.

Fauzia was not a morning person. She used to wake up late and not do a thing, all day she would either argue with everyone or have Ayesha do her massages. Her mother-in-law had started to realize how helpful Amna was but did she express it? No. She still did not care because as long as all the house chores were being done, she had nothing to worry about. She had not married her son to Amna rather she had got a silent maid for her house. Amna knew she had to do something to change everything. She could not bear to see her daughter suffer like this. She had to take a step. But what could she have possibly done; she was helpless with no other place to go. She had to end herself and her dreams, her hopes, her wishes to have a roof above her head. She had to forget what comfort or peace was so that her daughter would not get homeless.

Amna did not have anywhere to possibly go; even her brother had told her that the doors to his house were shut for her now, Haya was too young and Shazia was married to a flirtatious man Amna hated. She had to act wisely; wiser than her mother-in-law. She was daisy but she had to turn into a poison ivy. She was a rose but now she was a petal less stem full of thorns. She had changed; physically and mentally. She was strong; ready to battle anyone who tried to take her daughter away from her. Her beauty had disappeared with all her care of what people would think, all her fears had gone along her beauty. All the terrors she had seen upon herself had turned her into what she had become. She was always the one who cared for everyone one, who loved life, who was very sentimental, who loved her haters but now that had changed. She had seen the bitter ugly side of this life and she had learnt how to deal with it over time.

Ayesha's birth was just like the birth of a slave born to serve Amna's in-laws. From doing the dishes all day to doing all the laundry; she had to do all chores at the young age of twelve. Amna decided she was going to use her education to make her life better. She was not highly qualified but she could at least teach kinder garden. She went to her mother-in-law and said, "Ms. Shaida?" Her mother-in-law had told her to call her that. Amna always wanted a friendly mother-like mother-in-law and so she always wanted to call her mother-in-law 'mother' but her mother-in-law had strictly forbidden her from calling her 'mother'. Amna stopped for a while as she waited for her mother-in-law's reply. He mother-in-law was having her British milk tea. She put the cup aside on her round table next to the couch she was sitting on in the living room and said, "Continue." Amna said, "I was wondering if I could do a job as a teacher; I will earn money to make our financial states better. I will also do all the house chores and now that Ayesha knows how to do most of the house chores, she could help me as well."

Her mother-in-law stared at her until she completed what she wanted to say and then thought quietly for a moment. She looked at her and said, "Ok, you can; but only as long as you bring all the money to me." Amna agreed. She had a plan. Her mother-in-law could never have seen what was coming her way. She just wanted money; no matter how much she got, she still wanted more. She let Amna do her job thinking Amna would work all day and then give her all her pay.

Amna knew she had to submit her documents; her graduation certificate and other important documents so she started to look for them all around the house. She looked for them everywhere; in her cupboards, in her drawers, in her closets; everywhere but they could not be found by her anywhere. She was tensed. Those documents were the only way her life could have became a little better and now they were lost as well. She was panicking, she had to find them at all costs otherwise she knew that her daughter's life would become worse than hers for she at least enjoyed her childhood but Ayesha could not even do that. Amna had to find them even at the cost of her life.

The whole day was spent in finding the papers by Amna. The next day, she had to do the same thing today; she had the same objective until she succeeded. She again looked in the whole house; there was one place she had skipped before, she had not checked her suitcase she had bought with her on her marriage. She took a deep breath, bent down and pulled out a big brown suitcase from below her bad. She blew on it as she blew off all the dust off the matt suitcase. She slowly popped open the two metal locks in front of the suitcase. She then slowly lifted the upper side of the suitcase up and looked down to see some of her old fancy embroidered cloths that her friends and family had gifted her on her wedding. She started to pick up each clothing item and looked under and around it to see if the documents were there. She had lost all hopes when she put aside her last cloths in the suitcase and saw that there was nothing under them. She threw her head down in disappointment and slowly started to close the suitcase.

Suddenly, some papers slipped out of a silk pocket on the top side of the suitcase as Amna was closing the suitcase. S he had not noticed that pocket before. She quickly and enthusiastically took the papers in her hands and went through them. After she had realized that those were the documents she had been looking for, she smiled as she let out a sigh of relief as she put the documents close to her. She held them close to her chest as if she hugged them for some time as she had a vision of her life becoming better in her mind. She just imagined her daughter having all what she did not. The next day, as she had planed; she went out in search of a school. Their house was in a deserted low populated area and was quite far from any public place so Amna had to either take a cab or walk for miles. She did not have any money with her so her only option was to walk. She thought, "Well a little hard work is not a bad deal for a life changing opportunity" as she started to walk out of her street.

Almost an hour later, she was finally in the main public area. She was not used to all this; busy roads, rushing cars, crowds of people but she had to get used to it. She hesitantly and slowly walked up to a woman next to her who was buying vegetables from a green grocer. She slowly tapped her shoulder to get her attention. The woman was quite obese and wore an embroidered cream colored chador with deep red embroidered edges. She had loosely wrapped the chador around her round head. She turned around to face Amna as she picked up her vegetables in a plastic bag from the shop's counter. Amna asked, "Excuse me ma'am, I wanted to know if there are any schools in the nearby area." The woman was luckily very nice and directed Amna to the school just be the end of the road. Amna thanked her as she walked in the school. She asked for directions to the main office from several people inside the school until she was finally outside the main office. She knocked on the brown wooden door that had a thin metal plate on it that read, "Main Office". She waited for any response. After a while of silence, she knocked again and slightly opened the door and stepped in. She felt the cold air conditioner air hit her face as she walked in the room. Coming from the intense summer heat of the sun, this room felt like heaven to her.

She looked to her left and saw that a middle aged woman was working with some papers on her desk. Amna walked up to her and said, "Excuse me, I am here to find a job; is there a need of a teacher in any small class; kinder garden maybe?" The woman asked her to sit down on the soft leather chair next to Amna. Amna sat down. The woman asked, "You are just in time. We needed a teacher to teach students of grade one. It is as easy as teaching kinder garden children but the pay will be a bit more. All you need to do is submit all your documents, your ID card, your graduation certificate, your matriculation certificate etc and if we feel that you are right for the job, we will call you in a day."Amna was happy but at the same time she was worried whether they were going to call her or not. She went back home after a long and tiresome walk and spent the next hour praying and crying in front of her God.

That night, Amna could not sleep. She had broken sleep all night long. Ayesha asked the reason for this but her mother did not want to tell her what she had planned to do. The night passed, the next morning, Amna woke up and impatiently ran to the mail box. She did not want anyone to see if she had been or had not been taken on the job. She opened the mail box and to her delight, there was a letter inside it, addressed to her from the school. They had asked her to come to the school for her interview. Amna was beyond happy; this had to be the turning point in her life. She thought that she was finally going to be able to change everything. She was going to give her daughter the life she never had. Everything was going to be changed.

CHAPTER TWELVE

Amna took the letter in her hands and smiled as she ran to her mother-in-law's room. She stopped outside the door and knocked on it thrice. She took a deep breath and waited. Her mother-in-law allowed her to come in. Amna slowly walked in and said, "Ms. Shaida, I have got the job where I had applied. Can I go there today for my interview?" Shaida allowed her; she knew as soon as Amna would start the job, she will get the money and that was all she wanted.

Amna did very well understand what her mother-in-law wanted and why she had allowed her to go for the interview but she thought as long as she could do this job, all was fine. This was the very first time someone was tricking Shaida. She hated Amna just because she was Tariq's daughter. This was her revenge; the tortures she did on Amna were her revenge on Tariq and she had been successful up till now but that was all about to change. She did not understand that what goes around comes back around; what one does that happens to him as well.

Amna's plan was not to just do the job and make her financial crises end. Instead she had something much, much more complex, planed. She took her chador and began her journey of miles on foot to the school. I n an hour or so, she was there. She again went directly to the main office to meet the same woman she had met before. The woman sat on her seat next to her desk. She asked Amna to come in and sit on the chair next to her.

After she had settled down, the woman said, "As I already know your name and qualification; I am not going to waste my time asking you such information. Rather tell me if you have had any experience with teaching or children before?" Amna nervously gulped and said, "Actually I have never done any kind of job my entire life, this is going to be my very first experience. I have had a daughter and a son in the past but unfortunately both died; my son fell off the roof and my newborn daughter died mysteriously. I know this would not put a good impression on you but I think you had to know this. Ii currently have a daughter, Ayesha Tand she is almost twelve." The woman nodded lightly as she continued, "Very well, Can you tell me, why you want this job?" Amna slowly said, "I need this job for certain reasons but the top most being my daughter; I need to give her a better life." The woman asked, "Are you a single mother?" Amna smiled and replied, "Well not actually but you can consider that. I think there are a few things I want to tell you. My husband is not very supportive or loving; even towards his daughter. He hits us both. It was fine when I was alone but now that they have started to do the same to my daughter, I can't bare it. I want to do this job so that my daughter can study." The woman stared at Amna for a while and then said, "Ok Amna, very well. I don't think you would be suitable for this job; you can try in some other school. I am sorry." Amna sighed and said, "No problem ma'am" as she got up and began to walk towards the exit. She twisted the door knob as she slowly opened the door sadly.

She had almost gone out as she heard her name being called. She turned around to see that the woman who had interviewed her was standing at her desk and calling her. Amna thought she might have left something on the desk so she walked back to her and asked, "Yes ma'am?" The woman smiled at Amna as she said, "Amna, I was joking. You have your new job; you can start coming from tomorrow on wards." Amna was beyond blissful. She was completely hopeless and then suddenly that woman had lit her up with hope and happiness. Amna eyes filled up with tears. The woman smiled for she knew that Amna was not sad but happy. That woman was actually the owner and the principal of that very school.

Amna wiped away her tears as she dearly thanked the principal. Amna had to work on her plan now, she said, "Ma'am, I have a little request. Would it be possible if you can save some of my pay with you and not tell anyone about it? I want to get separated from my husband but I have nowhere to go and when the saved money with you will be enough, I will buy a small apartment for me and my daughter. I hope you can understand a mother's struggle and pain." The woman looked down and said, "Amna... I don't think it would be possible because of the school policy..." Amna said, "Oh ok, then I will look for some other way." The principal looked at Amna and said, "Well you know what, I am the owner so I can do whatever I want. I will try my best to help you out!" Amna's frown tuned to a wide smile as the principal hugged Amna. Despite her being a stranger, she acted more like a family member than her own.

Amna said good bye as she left the school. It was almost evening so Amna had to hurry home before it turned dark outside. She rushed to her home and got there in less time than usual. Her mother-in-law was curious to know if she had got the job or not so she asked Amna about it. All she wanted was money. Amna told her that she had got the job and she was going to join from tomorrow. Her mother-in-law made it clear to her that she was going to take all of Amna's pay from her. Amna had already taken care of that problem so she did not fret. She then went to her room and told the whole situation to her daughter Ayesha. She told Ayesha of her plan as well which made Ayesha happy to some extent for even though they hated her and treated her like an animal, she had still lived with them from her whole life and had developed a one sided bond with them. Amna told her that the next few years were going to be crucial for them both but then they were going to enjoy the rest of their lives. Amna was finally content that everything was going to get better. **It was getting better.**

CHAPTER THIRTEEN

Six cruel years for Amna and Ayesha had passed. Ayesha was now eighteen now and Amna was thirty one. Khalid had grown so old that he could not work anymore. His second wife, Fauzia on the other hand was older to Amna but much younger to Khalid. Khalid had married women almost half his age and it was something that was acceptable in society for a man to do.

Ahtasham and Nadia had been married and they both were lading a successful life. They both had bought their separate homes and had decent jobs. Khalid's mother had died of old age. She died a painful death; instead of dying seeing her son respect and care for her she saw her son contribute to her death. Amna kept on caring for her mother-in-law despite all that she had done to her when she could.

Till her last breath, Amna was by her side and

luckily she asked for Amna's forgiveness before she died. Amna knew that if she did not forgive Ms. Shaida now, maybe someone might not forgive her when she is helplessly lying on the death's bed. She forgave her mother-in-law; she forgave the woman who had killed her mother when she was young, she forgave that woman. Amna was still doing the same job but now was teaching a higher class. On a crisp December morning, Amna got up and got ready to go to her job. She now could afford a cab by herself; it was not that big of a change but for her things had gotten better a lot already. She got to the school and into her class and started to teach her class of fourth graders. Mid class, she was called into the Principal office. She did not know why the principal, who was also a supportive and great friend of Amna, had called her in her office. Anyway she went there and the principal hugged her as soon as she entered the room. She said, "Amna, I have good news" as she pulled out a stack of money from one of the drawers in her desk and continued, "Amna, the money you asked me to save for you is now enough for you to buy an apartment next to mine. The reason I did not tell you this before was because two years earlier, the money was only enough for you to buy a low class old apartment but now you can afford a luxury apartment next to mine." Amna put her hand on her mouth as she laughed in joy and quickly hugged the principal again. Amna started to cry. All that had happened to her and her daughter circled her mind. She was happier than ever. Her fate had finally favored her. She was finally going to end all hers and her daughter's pains and troubles. Back at Khalid's house, they financial crises had not ended and did not seem like they were going to end for a very long time but Amna's life was about to take a complete turn. She was brave, courageous and independent now; everything that she did not even think she was going to become when she was sixteen. Amna asked the principal if she had seen any vacant for sale apartments and the principal said yes; there was one right next to hers. Her life could not have gotten better. She made a deal with the owner of the building and bought it. The apartment was fully furnished and big enough for having a whole family of six in it. Amna did not tell this to anyone back at home.

She told this big news to her daughter who was ready to move out of that dungeon. One day, Amna took Ayesha to school with her and told everyone that the principal had called her. This was going to be the day Amna and Ayesha were going to move out of that house. The principal was really supportive and she helped Amna throughout her journey; Amna could not have thanked her enough. Amna and Ayesha moved into their new apartment; they did not need anything from their previous 'home' for they had everything they needed with them. Amna went to her lawyer and asked him to prepare the paperwork for hers and Khalid's divorce.

Everyone at Khalid's house was curious to why Amna and Ayesha had not come home by evening. It was not until night came that everyone really questioned their location. But they still did not care; who was going to ask about them? No one. So no one really cared if Amna and Ayesha came home or not; they did not even care if they were alive or not.

The next morning, there was a letter in the mail box. Fauzia went through them and realized that they were divorce documents. This was what Fauzia always wanted; she got very happy. Khalid did not care anymore; he divorced Amna. The only problem was that now they had to get a maid or a servant because they had just lost two. Khalid and his family of Fauzia and her two children surfed financial crises so much that it was difficult for them to live. Fauzia left Khalid and married another wealthier man; Khalid had now realized how big mistakes he had made when he was young but it was impossible for him to go back and time and change it all. He died a slow, regretful, painful and sad death.

On the other hand, Amna and Ayesha were happier than ever; living their best life. Finally Amna started to love life again. Amna continued her job and had a promotion; she now became the Head Urdu department. Ayesha was studying in that same school but was a class or two behind her age for she had skipped her studies when she was young. Amna was now independent and happier than ever. She now believed that **IT GETS BETTER.**

ABOUT THE AUTHER

The author of the book "IT GETS BETTER" is a first time author, Yasir Mazhar. The thirteen year old has had written several books in the past but never decided to publish any of them up till now. This thirteen year old male has always had a will to change the world. He had always supported equal rights for both women and men alike. This novel is written by him to show how much education and being independent is important for women. He has always been a feminist and so has always supported women rights.